LOIS LENSKI

TO BE A LOGGER

Other Books by Lois Lenski

J

TO BE
A LOGGER

by

Lois Lenski

J. B. LIPPINCOTT CO.

Philadelphia New York

1967

For my
beloved
Forest Children

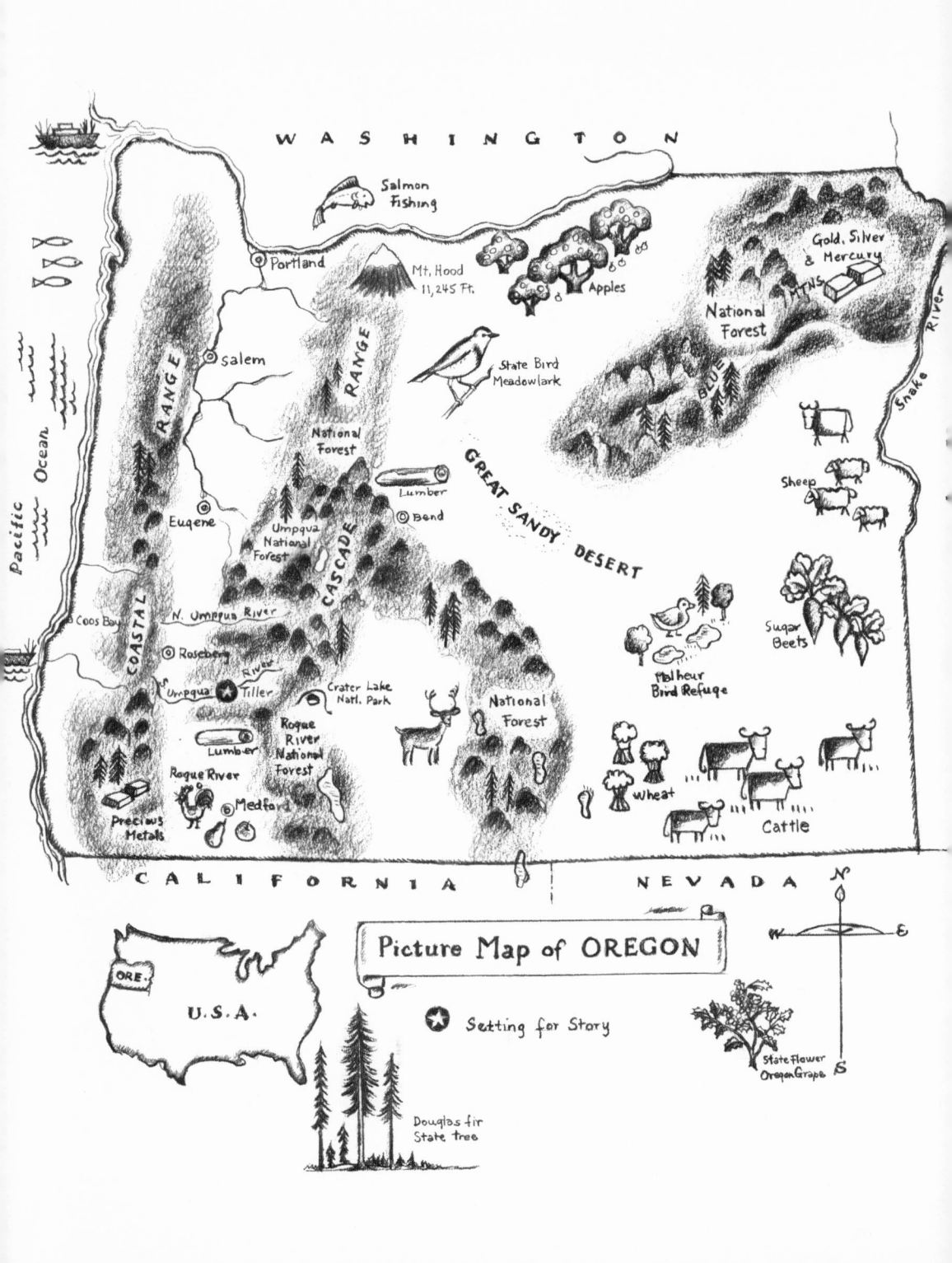

Picture Map of OREGON

Contents

Foreword

In the winter of 1957-1958, I had letters from five different locations in Oregon, inviting me to come to Oregon to write a logging story. Teachers and children there wanted to be represented in my Regional Series. Several of the locations sounded promising, and I exchanged letters with the children for a time. But unfortunately, due to illness in my family, I was unable to follow up by traveling to Oregon. So all my contacts were lost.

Other projects for other books intervened, but the idea for an Oregon logging story was never forgotten. I collected what material I could find and I read books on Oregon, but found little or no information on how a logger's family really lives. Not until 1966 was I free to entertain the thought of a trip to Oregon. I knew, from the past experience of writing all the other books in the Regional Series, that the only way to get the material was to go to the region and get it firsthand from the people living there, and to get my own impressions through my own eyes, ears, mind, and feelings.

One of my previous correspondents had been Mrs. Portia Shiltz, editor of the Myrtle Creek Mail, *a small weekly newspaper. I wrote to her to renew our acquaintance, and with the help of a small news item in the* Mail, *I began to receive more Oregon letters. One of the first came from Viola Rogers of Drew Rural Station, Tiller, Oregon. Mrs. Rogers wrote:*

"I run a country store and my husband has a gas station. All our friends are loggers . . ."

That was enough. Instinctively I felt this was the place I wanted to go. When Mrs. Rogers offered the hospitality of her home as a base for my stay while doing my field work, I felt more certain than ever that the choice was the right one. I never regretted the choice.

In June of 1966 I flew to San Francisco, where I was met by Celeste Frank, the former Iowa teacher who had helped me get material for Corn-Farm Boy. She offered to go with me, drive a car for me, and help in every way possible. We flew from San Francisco to Medford, Oregon, where the Rogerses met us. They drove us fifty miles, over our first Oregon mountain, to Drew and to their home.

Then began many happy adventures. My time was short, I had hard work to do and I had to work fast. My days were crowded, filled with new experiences, new people, and a completely new way of life. As always in other regions, everyone was eager and anxious to help.

With Mrs. Frank as a congenial companion, I attended the Rooster Crow contest at Rogue River, visited Skeeters' Logging Camp at Prospect, toured the Oregon Veneer Mill at White City, interviewed Mrs. Al Cooper, the grandmother logging-truck driver at Shady Cove, and rode on a logging truck myself with Bob Bonney from the logging location in the forest 3500 feet high for 135 miles round trip to the mill at White City. Besides interviewing logging families, I made sketches, took photographs and helped Mrs. Frank collect specimens of Oregon trees, flowers, and shrubs.

The families who contributed generously were: Glann Rogers, Joe Zimmerman, Ralph Stauch, Joe Crumpton, Richard (Bob) Bonney, John Niemela, Al Cooper, Ray Norris, Jim L. Jenks, Clair Henry, and Cliff Hughes. To them all and their children go my sincere thanks for making this book possible.

In many ways, it has been one of the most difficult of my Regional books to write. The technical information regarding the several methods of logging has been difficult to absorb and to simplify to a degree whereby it would not overload the story interest. Yet this concrete information telling just how the logging is done must be a vital part of the story especially for boy readers. So it could not be omitted.

I had anticipated that it might be difficult to tie up the men's occupation to family life and the children's interests, but here I was agreeably surprised. In perhaps no other Regional that I have written is the father's occupation more fully shared by wife and children. They all literally live *logging. They eat and sleep logging all the year round just as I have been doing while writing and illustrating this book.*

There is an appeal about logging, about the whole story of the big woods and what has happened to it over the years, the drama of its disappearance at the hands of man's greed, and the long slow course of his coming to a realization of his folly, and a determination to rectify his mistaken policies and do what he can to bring the forests back to Oregon. I hope it is not too late—although scenes of desolation on logged-off mountainsides have left a scar on my memory never to be erased. By way of contrast with the majesty and grandeur of those portions of the forests still left intact, surely one of the most magnificent of God's creations, one cannot help but wish that man had come to his senses sooner, that the lust for money had not so dominated the lumber companies' objectives to the exclusion of all other values.

One must remember that logging is a way of life to the people who live it and depend upon it for their well-being. To them the cutting of trees is not a tragedy, but an occupation, a means of earning money to pay for food and consumer goods. It is the only way of life they have ever known and being in it and of it, it is hard for them to see it as objectively as the outsider can.

All the logging that I witnessed and heard about was being done on National Forest land. I heard many conflicting opinions regarding Forest Service policies and practices, expressed by honest men who know the woods and have worked in it all their lives as their ancestors did, and whose way of life is bound up in the forest. I heard more antagonism than approval of Forest Service practices. The loggers are better able to judge these matters than I, an outsider and casual but keenly interested observer. I have expressed no opinion of my own, but have merely acted as a reporter, setting down what I heard.

Incidentally, the Forest Service men are not called "rangers" in this area. In fact, I was told that if you called one of their men a "ranger," he would be sure you were from back east or would "drop dead with shock."

To be a logger *or not to be, is a question every boy in the logging areas will have to decide for himself. There is no doubt there is a pull and a fascination about the occupation which can get into the blood- stream of some, while others will turn away from it.*

Logging is in a period of transition.

Besides the actual cutting and harvesting done by man, other forces —fire, disease, and insects are also working for the destruction of the forests. This means that logging as done in the past is nearing an end, and that man's work in the woods will in the future take on a different character. The answer, therefore, for the true forest lover, can be only the one chosen by my hero—a constructive approach. Lumbering, too, has changed, has lately become so diversified and has created so many new jobs, it is certain they will attract the boys of the area in the years to come. That, of course, is a different story.

As in my other Regionals, learning to know and trying to understand a new way of life has been a rich and rewarding experience, and I thank my many Oregon friends for making it possible.

Lois Lenski

August 14, 1966

DEFINITIONS

A-frame—simple log frame in shape of letter A, to which cables and pulley are attached for lifting small logs.

Binders—fastenings used to tighten the chains that hold the logs in place on the logging truck.

Bucker—logger who saws (or bucks) a log into shorter lengths.

Calk Shoes (or boots)—heavy loggers' boots, usually twelve inches high, with spikes in soles, for walking in woods on steep and slippery ground.

Cat—any tractor of track-laying or caterpillar type, used to pull logs to the landing; also clears off and makes logging roads.

Cat-skinner—logger who operates a track-laying tractor.

Chaser—man who unhooks chokers at spar-pole.

Choker—length of heavy cable on one end of which is a "bell," on the other end a nubbin, which hook together around a log to move it.

Choker-setter—logger who fastens a choker around a fallen log, so it can be yarded or dragged.

Copenhagen—a form of chewing tobacco popular with loggers.

Crummy—small car or bus, often yellow, owned by lumber company, used to transport loggers to woods.

Donkey—a diesel engine which controls the cables which bring the logs to the landing.

Donkey-puncher or donkey-engineer—logger who operates the donkey.

Faller—logger who saws trees down with power chain saw.

Fall a tree—current usage in Oregon for to *fell* a tree. *Fall* is used as a transitive verb.

Gyppo loggers—contract logger or small independent operator. The word does not denote "gypping."

High climber—logger who climbs and tops the highest trees, which are used for spar-poles, and hangs rigging in them for the setting.

High lead—logging which uses lifting power of high rigging to get logs up and over obstructions on the way from woods to landing.

Hooker or hook-tender—the boss of the rigging, or yarding crew in high lead logging.

Homelite—trade name of a particular chain saw.

Landing—place where logs are assembled for loading.

Powder monkey—logger who handles dynamite and blasts rock for roads.

Shovel—diesel and gas shovel for loading logs onto logging trucks.

Shovel-operator—logger who operates the shovel.

The show—a logging outfit.

Skid road—log road over which logs were skidded out of the woods in early days.

Snag—standing dead tree in forest.

Spar-pole—tall tree left in place, topped and stripped of branches, to which all rigging is (cables are) attached.

Spud—tool used to scrape or peel bark off cut logs or posts.

Stagged pants—loggers' pants cut off above calk boot tops and fringed, so they will not catch on anything.

Swede—a three-foot extension handle used on the binders.

Tin hat—hard hat worn by loggers for protection. Made of aluminum, plastic, or laminated paper—anything but tin.

Tin pants—heavy, water repellant duck pants worn by loggers in rainy weather.

Widow-maker—branch from a dead tree which may fall on a man's head and make his wife a widow.

Winch—a drum at the back of a cat on which the cable is wound.

Yamaha—trade name of special motorcycle.

Yarding—moving logs to a central spot.

SONG OF THE FOREST CHILDREN

We walk in the forest
   when the wind is still;
Not a branch moves,
   not a sound until
A squirrel jumps up—
   a flash of brown,
And a flood of pine cones
   goes tumbling down.

We run from the forest
   when the wind blows wild;
Down fall dead branches
   o'er rotten logs piled.
Snake, squirrel, and rabbit
   show no fear,
The forest their refuge
   when danger is near.

We sleep in the forest
   beneath giant trees;
Ghostly the moonlight,
   chilly the breeze.
The screech owl hoots
   and the chipmunks play
Over our heads
   as night turns to day.

TO BE A LOGGER

Chapter One

THE BOY

"CORK boots! I want cork boots!" cried Little Joe.

Dad sat on the wood-box, greasing his boots. Calk boots, called "cork boots" were twelve inches high and had sharp spikes all over their soles. Little Joe wanted to wear them and go stumping through the house like Dad.

"Makin' splinters on the floor!" scolded Mom.

Everybody laughed at Little Joe and teased him.

"Your feet are too little, they'd fall off!" said Dad.

"You're plumb cuckoo!" jeered Jinx.

"A fine logger you'll be, 'fraidy cat!" teased big sister Sandy.

But Little Joe kept on coaxing.

"Cork boots! The very idea!" said Mom, her lips pressed tight.

"You'll never get a pair—I'll see to that. I'm not raisin' my son to be a logger, that's for sure."

Dad just laughed.

"Loggin's in his blood, Nellie, don't forget that. You're not gonna make him a sissy-pants, if I have my way about it."

Little Joe did not get the boots, but he kept on wanting them.

Little Joe's father was a logger. He was called Big Joe Bartlett because he was so big and strong and husky.

Little Joe, whose real name was Joel, lived with Mom and Dad and his two sisters in a log house built by Granddad. It stood on a rise of ground above a small creek in southwestern Oregon. A bumpy dirt road ran along by the creek out to the highway. All around were mountains covered with a dense forest of trees.

Little Joe loved to climb trees. He climbed his first tree when he was only two. He ran out of the house and climbed a tree to get away from Mom. She came after him with a switch, but he only climbed higher.

"You little monkey!" she scolded. "Come right down here."

But he did not come.

She threw away her switch and still he did not come. Then she saw that he was scared. And he did not know how to get down. She had to lift him down.

When he was five, Dad gave him an axe. So he began to chop trees down. He took a small saw of Dad's and bucked (sawed) the trees into logs. He rolled the logs down the hill and watched. He laughed when they splashed into the creek.

"He's a little logger, for sure!" bragged Dad.

Billy Weber was Little Joe's best friend. Little Joe looked up to Billy because Billy was two years older than he. Billy had long shaggy hair and freckles on his nose. He was always barefoot in summer and his clothes were ragged. He lived over on the other side of the ridge, but he took a shortcut to Little Joe's house. He came any time and was never in a hurry to go home.

Billy liked chopping trees down just as Little Joe did. His father was a logger, too, and he knew little else.

One day Billy and Little Joe went off up the hill, carrying their axes. They walked a while looking at trees on the way. Then they chose one and stopped.

"I'll make a bet with you," said Billy. "You chop it down . . ."

Little Joe listened.

"I bet you can't chop it down by the time I climb up to the top and back down again," said Billy.

"O.K.," said Little Joe. "Go ahead. I'm a fast chopper. You'd better watch out."

Billy started climbing and Little Joe began chopping the tree. He chopped faster and faster and the chips went flying. Soon the tree began to lean. It cracked loudly. Little Joe jumped out of the way just in time. It fell with a loud *galump* and a noisy rustle of the branches.

Little Joe won the bet. But where was Billy? He had climbed to the top, but hadn't got back down again. Little Joe dropped his axe and stared.

"Where are you, Billy?" he called in a weak voice.

He could not see him anywhere and there was no answer. A squirrel jumped out of the tree and ran away.

"Billy!" called Little Joe, panic-stricken. Was he mashed underneath?

Then Dad was suddenly standing there beside him. He hadn't heard Dad come up at all.

"Billy is . . ." Little Joe began. "He's underneath."

Dad pushed the branches aside. There was Billy underneath, laughing. He wasn't hurt at all. He was only pretending.

"Let's do it again!" cried Billy.

But Dad said no, he might get hurt.

Little Joe learned a lot from Billy. Billy took him for hikes in the woods, the dogs at their heels. There was big, old lazy Ringo, the cow-dog, part Collie; mean little Corky, half bulldog, half-terrier; and Rex, just plain cur. All the loggers had plenty of dogs and most of them were mean. Oregon was a country of big trees, big logs, and big dogs.

One day Little Joe and Billy came to a clearing of wild grass. They heard some yapping, but it was not the dogs. The boys stood still and listened.

"Gray diggers!" said Billy. "Let's go up quiet."

There they were, the digger squirrels. They were eating seeds off the wild grass. They were standing up, the tall grass between their legs. They filled the pockets in their cheeks with seeds.

"Cute little fellas, ain't they?" said Little Joe. "Sometimes I see them at the barn getting oats, or under the big oak tree, munching acorns."

"They got tunnels in the grass," said Billy. "They make long runs and fill 'em up with acorns and seeds and stuff to eat in winter. Wish I'd brought my gun along."

"What do you want to shoot 'em for?" asked Little Joe.

"Oh, just for the heck of it."

Suddenly out from the brush jumped the dog Corky. Before either of the boys could say a word, he grabbed the biggest digger squirrel by the neck, as the others disappeared in the burrows.

Little Joe yelled and Billy grabbed at the dog. The dog dropped his prey. The squirrel lay on the ground, not moving. Little Joe brought it home on a stick, dropping it twice.

"It's just knocked out," he kept saying.

But it wasn't.

"It's plumb dead," said Dad, when he met them on the path.

They made a hole and buried it.

"Corky's worse'n a hawk!" cried Little Joe, furious. "I'll beat the living tar out of him!"

He found a stick and chased after the dog. The dog ran to the house, yelping as if he had been killed. What a coward he was, after all. His yelps brought the girls out of the house, screaming. Jinx, long legs and long hair flying, and back of her Sandy, red hair in curlers, waving one of Mom's aprons.

"You're cruel!" yelled Jinx. "Let my dog alone!"

"Don't you touch Corky again or I'll clobber you!" shouted Sandy.

Billy stood and watched, mouth wide open. He had no sisters, so did not know what to expect next.

Suddenly the rumpus was all over. The girls dropped Corky and went indoors. Little Joe went off with Dad to feed the hogs, so there was nothing for Billy to do but go home.

One day Little Joe and Jinx were loading house wood. Dad had falled a madrone tree, sawed off the limbs, bucked them in chunks, and split them. The children had to pile the wood in the pick-up. Madrone wood was good for firewood. It held the heat a long time and left few ashes.

Jinx was younger than Little Joe. Her hair was long and always in the way. She often wore shorts and a T-shirt. She was a tomboy and liked doing all the things Little Joe did.

"What we need is a donkey to load this wood," said Jinx. She threw a piece of wood into the truck angrily.

"A donkey?" asked Little Joe.

"Yes," said Jinx, "like the loggers have, to load logs."

Little Joe stared at her. *"Donkeys don't load logs!"* he said.

"Yes, they do, and so do cats!"

Little Joe said, "I don't believe you."

Jinx told everybody at the supper table.

"Little Joe says donkeys don't load logs! And cats don't either!"

They laughed, Dad most of all.

"I'm glad he don't know," said Mom. "There's plenty of things he's better off without knowing."

Dad looked at his son, disappointed and a little sad.

"Son," he said, "there's two kinds of donkeys, and only one has four legs. Jinx meant the other kind. A donkey, to a logger, is a machine. So is a cat."

Little Joe looked at the floor, ashamed.

"It's time you went to the woods with me," Dad said. "A good logger knows how to do anything in the woods. He can fall and buck trees, he can operate the donkey, the cat, or the shovel. He can top a tree and put up rigging. It's time you learned about some of these things."

Mom shook her head.

"I've lived all my life without seeing a logging operation," she said, "and I hope I never will."

But she did not say the boy could not go. She knew it would be a waste of breath. Big Joe was determined to make a logger out of Little Joe, no matter what.

Dad planned the trip the night before. He sent Little Joe to bed early.

"Wake up, Little Joe! You goin' with me?" he called next morning.

It was still dark and Dad was calling. Little Joe opened his eyes and jumped into his clothes. Mom, half awake, was pouring coffee. The girls were still in bed. Dad was at the table, eating bacon and eggs. Little Joe stuffed food into his mouth quickly.

He watched Dad put on his calk boots and his tin hat. Mom held
out the lunch bucket, then went back to bed.

Next thing Little Joe knew, they were in the old rickety Ford
bumping down the highway. A long ride down the twisty canyon road, with high rocky cliffs on one side and a steep drop
down to Elk Creek on the other. At the corner by River Bend
store and garage, Dad and Little Joe left the car and piled into
the crummy. It was just getting light.

The crummy was yellow and looked like a small bus. It had
seats facing the front, on both sides of a center aisle. It belonged
to the Elkhorn Logging Company and was used to take the crew
to work. Their cars were left parked by the garage.

The men piled into the crummy, laughing and joking.

"Little logger! Little logger!" they cried, teasing Little Joe.

"A chip off the old block!" they shouted, razzing Dad.

The road got bumpier and rougher as they left the River Road
and entered the National Forest. The crummy wound in and
around and up and down on a narrow trail through the mountains. Little Joe kept bobbing off to sleep and waking up
again.

At last they got there and the men jumped out.

Little Joe got out, too, and looked around.

Dad showed him the big caterpillar tractor and told him it
was called *the cat*. The choker-setter put a cable around a log
and hooked it to the drawbar behind the cat. Then the cat-
skinner pulled it to the landing.

It was fun to watch.

Little Joe knew now that cats and donkeys were not four-
legged animals, but powerful machines.

At noon the whistle blew and the men stopped work. They sat in the shade and ate their lunch. They laughed and joshed each other. They teased Little Joe and predicted he'd be a better logger than his dad.

It was a long day for Little Joe, but one he never forgot. That night he was very tired, but his logging education had begun.

Now he wanted to be a logger more than ever.

After that, every chance he got, he ran down the bumpy woods road to the highway. He wanted to watch the great logging trucks go by. The little creek crossed over the road in a culvert and emptied into Elk Creek back of the Drum Country Store. A great cliff jutted out into the highway across from the store, making a bad turn in the road. The trucks had to slow up going past.

Little Joe sat on a rock and waited. In the early morning, one truck came along after another. The men had all started loading at daylight. Each logging company had trucks of a certain color. Some were blue, others red, green, or yellow. Uncle Irv's was orange. He was a gyppo trucker. That meant he was independent. He owned and drove his own truck.

Little Joe waited. He heard a loud grinding roar. He looked up the highway—a logging truck was coming. He watched as it came closer. Was it Uncle Irv's? No, it was yellow.

He stood by the road and signaled, raising his arm, bent at the elbow. The driver answered, tooting his horn.

Whoo! Whoo! sounded the air horn. The truck drivers enjoyed signaling to small boys. Little Joe laughed.

What a huge thing it was! Sixty-five feet from front to back, carrying a stack of logs forty-eight feet long, resting on its trailer. Some of the logs were more than three feet in diameter. What big trees they must have been! Now they were on their way to the mill in town to be sawed into lumber. Round a bend, the truck was already out of sight, speeding along at fifty miles an hour.

Every time he saw Uncle Irv, Little Joe begged for a ride on his logging truck. When he was six, Uncle Irv took him for the first time. It was the biggest thrill he had ever had. After that, Uncle Irv took him often. He enjoyed the boy's company, and the boy like nothing better.

Every time Billy Weber came over, the boys talked about what they wanted to do when they grew up. It was always logging.

"When I get big," said Billy, "I'm gonna drive a cat."

"When I get big," said Little Joe, "I'm gonna drive a logging truck."

"Joel! Come here," Mom called one day.

He was always called Joel now, because he was twelve and growing up so fast. He had not been called Little Joe since he started to school at six years old.

"Take this letter down to the store and mail it," said Mom. "Get two loaves of bread, a pound of oleo, and a large can of beans. Tell Myra to charge it."

Joel snatched a biscuit off the table. He looked at the letter. It was addressed to Aunt Alice, Mom's sister, in Rogue River, Oregon. What was she writing to her for? He jumped on his bike and rode down to the highway. His bike was an old one, rescued off a dump, but it was still able to go. It was faster than walking or running, even.

Joel went into the store. Myra Ross, the owner, was sitting on a stool behind the counter reading a book. She didn't even look up. Joel went to the cubbyhole postoffice in the back and dropped the letter in the slot. Then he picked up his groceries. Bread from one shelf, beans from another, and oleo from the case. He plumped them down on the front counter and said, "Charge it!"

Still Myra did not look up.

Joel banged the can of beans down loudly and shouted, "I said *charge it!*"

Myra looked at him over her glasses and said softly, "I heard you the first time."

"If you didn't spend all your time reading books," Joel said in a loud voice, "you'd be a better storekeeper."

"That so?" asked Myra.

"Yes, and I mean it," said Joel.

The door opened and Billy Weber came in. He and Joel were still the best of friends.

"What's the matter with reading a book?" asked Myra.

Billy answered for Joel, "Loggers don't need to read books. My dad said so."

"Some loggers are afraid they might learn something," said Myra. "Good thing all boys' fathers are not loggers."

The two boys looked at each other. What a funny thing to say. Everybody knew that dads were always loggers.

"My father's a logger," bragged Billy.

"So's mine," said Joel. "And so's Jim Hunter's and Snuff Carter's and . . ." He rattled off the names of all the boys he could think of.

"But what about Andy Whitcomb?" asked Myra. "His father runs the River Bend gas station. And Roy Benton. His father brings the mail."

It was true. The boys had never thought of it before. She was right. The danged woman was always right. Myra Ross was always jolting them somehow.

"There's lots of things you could be," Myra went on. "Doctors, lawyers, scientists, explorers, editors, merchants, storekeepers, mailmen, garage owners . . ."

Joel and Billy stomped out of the store angrily.

"Thinks she knows it all, that woman!" said Joel.

"My dad says she's crazy!" added Billy.

Joel thought for a minute. "Is she?"

"Well, she's got crazy notions," said Billy, "and she don't know beans about logging."

"That's right," said Joel.

"Who'd want to be a mailman?" asked Billy.

"Or run a gas station?" added Joel.

"There's only one thing to be," said Billy.

"Loggers," said Joel.

That ended the matter.

Chapter Two

THE HOUSE

"GOLLY! We're gettin' company!" cried Joel.

Two cars came up the woods road and people began to pile out. Joel ran to meet them. It was Uncle Irv and Aunt Ella and their children, and Uncle Curt and Aunt Bertha with theirs. Uncle Irv and Uncle Curt were Mom's brothers. It was Sunday and they all came to spend the day.

The women brought food, so they cooked and fussed in the kitchen. Mom's biggest coffee pot was full and boiling over. The children ran in and out and kept getting underfoot. The men found a shady spot in the yard outside. They stretched out and talked. Joel sat down and listened.

"You been laid off?" Curt asked Big Joe. "Nellie said she thought so."

"No, I quit!" said Dad. "My boss knows too much for his own good. I got mad at him and quit."

"Nellie says she never knows what time you're comin' home or if you've took a new job or quit or what . . ."

Dad smiled, but did not answer.

"What you been doin' around here, Big Joe?" asked Irv. "A little loggin'? Looks kinda bare round the old house, don't it?"

The old log house, built by Granddad Bartlett, stood above the creek with trees around it. They had grown thicker and larger and bushier since Granddad's death, so the house had been getting shadier and darker. The ridge to the east kept the sun off in the morning and the ridge to the west kept it off in the afternoon.

Big Joe was like Granddad. He wanted the sun. So he began clearing the trees away. Cutting down trees was pure pastime. He did it because he enjoyed it.

"Guess I'm like my dad," Big Joe said. "Trees are something to cut—to be got rid of. When I want more sun, I fall 'em down!"

Curt and Irv laughed. They agreed. They were loggers, too.

Logging was Dad's way of life. He had learned it from Granddad and from all the neighbors—the old-timers and those his own age. Timber meant money in their pockets. Cutting trees was a means of subsistence, the way to keep their families from starving. They did not stop and ask themselves do I want to be a logger, or do I want to do something else. They were loggers and knew little else. Once a logger, always a logger.

Even Joel could understand that.

Dad had been clearing land for a long time. Whenever he came home early, or on Saturdays, or when he was laid off, he worked at clearing the land. He was not a man to be idle. He cleared the pastures for the cows and kept on clearing up the steep slope back of the house and far up the mountain on the next rise. There was an old log barn up there where he stored feed for the cows and fed them.

"When you gonna cut the big timber, Joe?" asked Irv.

"Or maybe you're gonna sell it for stumpage?" asked Curt.

Dad shook his head.

"I'm keepin' it," he said. "Keepin' it till I get my own show. Two hundred acres I got, the purtiest big timber you ever saw in your life. Purty nice nest egg, don't you think?"

The men agreed. They were in fact envious. They had not inherited any timber.

"I often think about the old man," Big Joe went on. "Mighty good of him to will me all that land, just when I come home from the Second World War all done out. Three hundred and twenty acres, a whole section—two hundred acres of it in good timber."

Joel liked to hear about Granddad. He sat as close to Dad as he could get, locked under Dad's arm. He listened, wide-eyed and wordless, drinking it all in.

Granddad was an old-time logger, who came to Oregon when it was still full of trees, virgin forests of giant trees, but to him and the early settlers they were just something to be got rid of. Granddad felt he was hemmed in by the mountains. As a boy he had lived in Nebraska and never knew what a mountain was. In Oregon, the mountains irritated him. He was closed in by the forest and could not see out. To him, logging was like skinning the fur off the side of the mountain, for the trees grew as thick as the hair on a dog's back.

Granddad's idea was: "Tear 'em out, cut 'em down, get rid of the forest. The trees are in the way, we can't see out. Whack 'em down, so we can see the blue sky and see off over them hills . . ." Funny then that he built his house down in the valley. Why didn't he build it up on top of the mountain? Was it too hard to get up there?

Granddad had cleared all he could, but the two hundred acres of timber were left intact. He had never got around to that. Two hundred acres of tall, beautiful timber in the Cascade Mountains, left to Dad as a legacy. Timber meant money, security. It was money in the bank. There it was waiting, timber for the taking.

Irv and Curt looked at each other.

"You're a rich man, Big Joe," said Irv.

"Nice job you'll have gettin' it out!" said Curt. "Gettin' it to market will be one whale of a job."

"I know," said Dad, soberly. "I'll get my own show. I'll do it myself."

"Where will you get the money?" asked Irv. "A cat with a dozer and a logging winch costs thirty-five thousand. You'll have to pay at least a third down."

"A lot of money for a logger," said Dad.

"Even for you?" asked Curt. "You makin' big money like you do, toppin' trees and gettin' the highest wages anybody gets?"

"Even for me," said Dad. "Taxes have to be paid on the timber or I'll lose it. A family to feed—and Nellie can't save a penny. She just lets money slip through her fingers . . ." But he did not like to talk to her brothers about that, so he stopped.

From that day on, Big Joe's goal was set. He made up his mind to keep that two hundred acres intact, no matter what happened.

Before he took another job with another outfit, he kept on clearing the hundred and twenty acres. Firewood was always needed and certain trees were better for that. Rail fences were built, a log hog pen and chicken coop were put together some-how, good enough to keep the winter rains out. Dad wanted the stuff cut off, to clear more pasture for the cows. Cut down the pines and firs, stash the brush and burn it. Get the stuff off. He kept on clearing and Joel helped him. Soon the boy could saw and chop like an expert. And he loved it, too, just as his father did.

Dad bought a cat, a small one, a bargain. Someone he knew couldn't keep up the payments, so Dad took it over. He set up an A-frame and began to get logs out faster. He rented a truck for short logs and hauled them himself. He showed Joel and the girls how to peel logs with a spud. The spud took the bark off the poles. The logs brought two hundred dollars more on a load if they were peeled.

Dad paid the children two cents a foot for peeling. They began to save their money.

The trees so close to the house still bothered Dad. He decided to clear them from the house to the creek. Saturday would be a good day to start. The evening before, Dad and Joel went down to look things over. They stared in surprise.

"You been fallin' trees here, son?" asked Dad.

"No," said Joel.

Several small trees were lying on the ground. They had been chopped off at the base and cut into chunks. There were other peeled branches lying around.

"*Sh!* Look! Beavers!" said Joel. "See the old one over there?"

There in the creek they saw him, pushing a branch ahead of him. On the bank stood the female gnawing a tree, with three little ones. They stood stiff like statues. Suddenly the big beaver whacked his tail and dived under. The next minute they were all in the water.

"They're pretty good fallers and buckers!" said Dad.

He pointed out skid roads where the beavers had been snaking the trees down to the river. Under its bank, they were storing the branches, to keep the bark green for future eating.

"Looks like the beavers want to help us," said Joel.

"Purty good loggers!" laughed Dad. "The whole creek needs clearin' out . . ."

"Don't clear out the beavers, Dad," said Joel.

"They'll just move farther down stream," said Dad. "I want to log all these trees off the side of the hill, to get more light in the house."

"When you log too many trees off, you get landslides," said Joel.

But Dad did not listen.

He worked that week at it and made good headway. He cleared out the creek, took the trees down and bladed off the bank with his dozer. Then a big rain came and he had to stop. It rained for three days. It poured and soaked the slippery clay ground. It rained so hard, it began to wash the hill and the house started to slide.

Mom and the girls were inside cooking supper. The house gave a jolt and Mom dropped the frying pan on the floor. She caught herself and held onto the cupboard. Jinx was peeling potatoes and Sandy was setting the table. They both took spills on the floor.

"Earthquake!" cried Mom, white in the face.

Dad came in soaking wet.

"Earthquake!" cried Mom again. "Did you feel it?"

"Hold your horses. Don't get excited," said Dad, calmly.

"But the house moved—I felt it!" cried Jinx.

"So did I!" cried Sandy.

Joel came in, drenched to the skin.

"The house slid, I saw it!" he announced. He sounded excited. "It moved a foot. It's starting to slide down hill."

"Glory!" cried Jinx. "I'm gettin' outa here!"

She ran toward the door.

"Come back here, girl," said Big Joe. "It's rainin' out. Stay inside and keep dry."

"But if we land in the creek," wailed Jinx, "we'll all get wetter."

"It's your fault, Dad," said Joel. " 'Cause you took off so much of the bank and logged those trees off the side of the hill. Now the house is going to slide right down into the creek."

Mom made a big fuss about it. Next day, Dad sunk some heavy logs down to hold the house, but after every rain it slid some more. It was the rainiest, wettest spring in years. More rains and the house slid off its foundations. Doors would not shut, the windows were crooked, the glass in them broke and big cracks came in the floor.

Mom wanted to move out right away. The barn was halfway up the mountainside. She threatened to move up there. But Dad paid no attention. He didn't seem to care.

He just kept on cutting trees down. Joel could think of only one reason why. It was the thing he liked to do best.

Mom wanted Dad to get back to work—something besides logging. She talked a lot about it. Couldn't he get some other kind of a job, so they could move to town and live there?

What else could Dad do, anyhow, if he changed jobs? Joel thought about it.

He could never be a carpenter, even if that meant working with wood. He could not even pound a nail in straight, Mom said. Look at that closet shelf he tried to put up. It was always coming loose and falling down.

He could never be a plumber. Look at those gravity pipes from that mountain spring. Dad had dug a big hole on the mountain side, higher up than the house, for the spring to fill up. It was to run of its own accord, an easy way to get water. But the pipes got busted. Mom said the cows tramped on them and Dad said it was the horses. Anyhow, the pipes got wrecked. Dad never rigged them up again, so there was no spring water to drink.

And the well with the electric pump . . . When the hillside slid, it broke the pipes and the well got covered up. Something got into it like diesel oil, and the water wasn't good any more. There was always the rain barrel at the side of the house. And down the road, across the highway by the store, there was a good spring, so water had to be carried after that in two big five-gallon cans.

When Mom talked about moving out, Dad began to talk about building a new house. For a long time now, he had been bringing in secondhand lumber in the pick-up. The Forest Service tore down a couple of old homesteads and Dad bought some of the used lumber and hauled it in. He bought used plumbing fixtures and dumped them in the yard around the house, too, along with old tires, window sash, broken wheels, piles of old rope, cans of paint, and other useful things. Dad had a plan of his own, all right. Other loggers in the area had salvaged used materials and were planning to build some day.

"What's all the junk for?" Mom asked. "You goin' in the junk business, Joe?"

Dad said, "Now you know, Nellie, I'm goin' to build us a nice new house . . ."

"Out of all that rotten lumber?" Mom laughed.

Dad said, "It's good wood."

"It'll take twice as long to pull the old nails out and get it in shape," Mom insisted.

"The boy can do that," said Dad, looking at Joel and grinning.

Each time, after a rain, when the house slid a foot or so, and a few dishes got knocked off the table, Mom complained and wanted to move.

Dad just said quietly, "We'll move when I get the new house built."

He really meant it, Joel could see that.

Mom would begin again, "How can you ever build a house when you can't pound a nail in straight?"

Dad did not like it. So he stomped out of the house, picking up his axe.

"Come on, Joel," he called in a loud voice.

He strode off up the hill like a great giant, with the three dogs barking at his heels. Joel took his axe and went along. He chopped, too, and helped pile up the brush.

No, you couldn't change Dad, Joel knew that. Even Mom with all her complaints never made a dent. Dad was what he was, a logger, and he'd never be anything else.

In June the rains stopped and a dry spell set in. The house stopped sliding halfway to the creek. A little willow tree held it.

Chapter Three

THE RATTLER

"DON'T you want to go, Joel?" asked Mom.

Joel hated town as much as he loved the woods.

"I won't ever go again," he said, "less'n you drag me."

"Don't go if you don't want to," said Mom.

"How about you, Jinx?" asked Sandy.

"Don't go, Jinx," said Joel. "Nothin' but smelly old stores . . ."

Mom and Sandy were going to town. It was fifty miles to Medford, all the way over a mountain and down on the other side.

Dad had a job again. He was hook-tender for the Johnson Logging Company. This was the kind of job he liked. He engineered the logging after he laid out the show. He told the crew what logs to bring to what place and saw that they did what they were told. He was making good wages and had had two paydays, so now Mom had money to spend. She and Sandy had a long list of things to buy.

"W'ell go to a show too," said Sandy.

Jinx looked at Joel and said, "No, I think I'll stay here. Too much trouble to put a dress on."

Dad was strict. He would not let the girls go to town in shorts, even if the weather was hot. Sandy said he was old-fashioned. But the girls had to mind.

Joel and Jinx had plans of their own. With Dad away in the woods and Mom and Sandy gone to town, they could do what they pleased. But first they had to drive the cows up to the mountain range, where they would stay for the summer. The range was land that Dad had leased from the Forest Service. Dad had given the children their orders the day before. If he told them to do something, they knew they had to do it or there would be trouble.

As soon as Mom and Sandy left in the car, Joel brought the horses out. The horses were old and decrepit. Dollie was seventeen years old and Star was twenty-one. They were so old they were terribly slow.

"Come on, Jinx, let's get going!" cried Joel.

"First I got to feed my pet trout," said Jinx.

She had bread and stale cake in her hands. She started running down the woods road.

"Where you going?" called Joel.

No answer, so he waited till she came back.

"They're still there," she said. "Under the culvert. They were hungry and glad to see me. I knocked some spiders off for them to eat, too."

"Well, come on," said Joel.

"They're rainbow trout, Joel, all colors of the rainbow," said Jinx.

"Come on, let's *go!*" cried Joel.

"Wait till I feed my banties," said Jinx, running to a pen near the woodpile.

"Gosh sakes!" cried Joel. "When we ever gonna get started?"

Jinx was raising a batch of baby banties. They had to be kept in a wire pen raised off the ground, so the coons and skunks would not get them. She also had a banty rooster and two hens that ran loose. The rooster's name was Rusty. They were Golden Seabrights. The rooster's feathers were black and gold. He had a double comb that was bright red.

"Did you put rouge on it?" asked Joel.

"Of course not," said Jinx. "Isn't he beautiful? You can hear him crow a mile away."

She fixed some mash for the baby chicks and threw some grain on the ground. Then she started for the house.

"Aw, come on!" begged Joel. "Where you goin' now?"

"To get *us* some food," said Jinx. "You don't want to starve, do you?"

She came out with a paper bag. In it were sandwiches of jelly and peanut butter, a banana, and a candy bar. At last she was ready to go.

They climbed on the horses and rounded up the cows in the

barnyard. There were eighteen of them and they all had names. Jinx knew every cow by name and rattled them off as they rode along.

"Red, Holly, Mandy, Butterball, Cricket . . . Open that gate, there, Joel! Watch out, Baldy's goin' the wrong way . . . Bun and Dot and Grumpy and Spotty and Crooked Face . . . Oh, I wish this horse would *move* . . ."

It was a hard job getting the cows to go up the mountain where they were supposed to go. Ringo, the cow-dog, was a big help, chasing them and nipping their heels. Rex ran back and forth, too. But the horses were slow and liked to stop and nibble grass. Coaxing and scolding and even slapping would not move them until they felt like going.

"I'm gonna get me a mustang!" said Jinx.

"Where?" asked Joel.

"From Wyoming," said Jinx. "They're only forty dollars and I'm saving my money. That's why I didn't want to go to town with Mom and Sandy today. I don't want to spend a penny. I'll get me a mustang—they're wild two-year-olds. They can gallop fast as lightning!"

"Who told you about them?" asked Joel.

"I saw an ad in the Medford paper," said Jinx. "It told all about the wild horses in Big Horn Canyon out in Wyoming."

"That's a long ways off," said Joel. "How would you get it here?"

Jinx had it all figured out.

"Dad would have to go after it with his pick-up," she said. "First, he'd have to rent a horse-trailer, though."

"It would be wild," said Joel. "Who would break it for you?"

"I'd break it myself," said Jinx. "I've read a lot of Westerns and I know just how it's done. There was an article in the *Farm Journal,* too: 'How to Break a Mustang in Half an Hour.' You put him in a cattle chute where there's scarcely room for him to move, then throw a saddle on him and cinch it up and let him kick as much as he can. He'll tame right down."

Joel laughed.

"Sounds easy," he said. "I hate these old nags. If Dad would get me a Yamaha motorcycle, I could come up here in half the time. They can go in rough places where horses can't walk."

"I'm gettin' saddle sore," said Jinx, "sittin' on this saddle so long."

When the children reached the range, they turned the cows in. They got off the horses and let them graze. Jinx and Joel wandered into the woods. It was cool and shady there under the big trees. They found a log and sat down to eat their lunch. They each had a sandwich, divided the banana, and Jinx ate the candy bar herself. Joel took his knife out of his pocket and began whittling twigs.

"I'd like to live in the woods all the time," he said. "I'd like to build me a cabin and shoot bear and deer to eat, and cook on a campfire like the Indians did."

"Live up here in the woods all by yourself?" asked Jinx.

"Yes," said Joel. "Once a year I'd go down to the store and buy matches and coffee and sugar . . ."

"You'd go cuckoo the way Old Indian John did," said Jinx.

"But I'd be happy . . . Sh! I hear something!"

"What is it, a bear?" asked Jinx.

"No, a bear's big and clumsy and makes a lot of noise," said Joel. "I've only seen one bear and it was dead—the one that Jed Allen shot and brought to River Bend gas station."

"When I was little, I thought I saw two bears up the road," said Jinx. "Till Dad told me they were Bentons' hound dogs."

"Sh! I hear the noise again!" said Joel.

The children listened. Above the chirping of the birds, a rustling noise could be heard. Joel looked on all sides, on the ground and in bushes and trees. Then he saw it—a porcupine up on the branch of a pine tree. The animal had puffed himself out to twice his normal size. His quills stuck straight out from his

body. He lashed his tail back and forth angrily.

"Don't go near him!" cried Jinx. "He'll throw his quills at you!"

"No, he won't," said Joel. "Gimme a stick. Porcupines don't throw their quills, you ought to know that."

Joel waved his stick.

"Wish he'd stop eating that tree. Porkies damage good trees that we want to log. They eat bark, acres of it."

A cloud passed over and the sun faded away. Suddenly the woods looked dark and dismal. There was a shadow behind every tree and a wild animal in every pile of brush, according to Jinx.

"Glory! Let's get outa here!" she cried, starting to run. "I don't want to meet a bear."

"No bears to be scared of, I told you," said Joel.

But Jinx was still running. At the edge of the woods she tripped and fell. Joel ran to help her. She was all tangled up in blackberry briars. Her long loose hair was caught in the vines. She twisted and turned, but only got tangled up worse than ever.

"Blackberries!" cried Joel. "Why didn't we bring a bucket?"

He began to pick them and stuff them into his mouth. They were sweet and delicious, as only wild Oregon blackberries can be.

"Help! Help! Get me outa here!" called Jinx.

The more she struggled, the more tangled up she became. Joel ran over to look at her.

"Guess you fell in head first," he said. "Your hair's got caught

and it's holding you tight." He pulled his knife from his pocket. "Wait! I'll cut it off!"

"Ouch!" screamed Jinx. "Let me loose! What you doin'?"

Joel cut again and again. At last he got his sister loose. He took her hand and pulled her out of the brambles. She was covered with scratches and blackberry juice.

"Look where you're goin' next time," warned Joel.

Jinx got to her feet and ate blackberries. Once she glanced down into the briars. Long strands of yellow hair lay there, a tangled mass.

"I never did like long hair anyhow," she said, tossing her head. "It's cooler in summer if it's short."

They went to the range and found the horses. Then they took off down the hill.

When they came back to the house, everything was quiet. They could hear the dogs barking in the distance. They had probably treed a coon or a skunk. No one was around. Mom and Sandy had not come back from town yet. Dad would not be home till late. The children sat on the doorstep and rested.

A rooster crowed loudly.

"That's Rusty, my Golden Seabright!" cried Jinx. "Don't you just love to hear him crow?"

"Hope this house don't slide any more," said Joel. "If it does, we'll land in the creek."

"We'll move in the new house Dad's going to build," said Jinx.

"Dad'll never get a new house built," said Joel.

Jinx stared at him. "How do you know?"

"I just know, that's all," said Joel. "Dad's too busy loggin'. He'll never take time off from loggin' to build a house. Come on, we'd better get some of that house wood in, so Mom can cook supper when she gets back."

Joel pointed to a pile of wood on the grass. Dad had dumped it from the pick-up. The wheelbarrow stood beside it.

"Dad said for us to get it in," said Joel.

"I don't feel like hauling in wood," said Jinx. "I'm tired. Besides, I'm hungry."

She ran into the kitchen and came out with a package of peanut cookies. She offered one to Joel and took two herself. The children sat on the step and munched cookies.

"See that big bird flyin' up there?" asked Joel, with his mouth full. "That's a red-tail hawk. Bet it's after digger-squirrels. I'll go in and get my gun." But he did not move.

Joel had a .22 rifle, but he did not use it often. He liked the animals in the woods and did not want to kill them. But he knew all about the rifle. At the age of six, Dad had taught him how to handle, clean, load, and fire it.

He went to the woodpile and began piling sticks in the wheelbarrow.

"Might as well get some wood in," he said, "or Dad will bawl me out when he gets home."

"Yes, you'd better," said Jinx, "if you don't want a good licking."

She went on munching cookies. She did not offer to help.

Joel bent over to pick up a chunky log and then jumped back. He heard a rattle, a nerve-tingling rattle. His face went white and he shook as if he had a chill.

"Snake! Snake!" he screamed, as soon as he could say the words. "It's a buzz-tail!"

Jinx jumped to her feet, frightened. She began to dance a jig.

"Where? Where? What'll I do?"

"Go climb a tree!" called Joel. "That's the safest place."

"There are no trees to climb," said Jinx. "Dad cut 'em all down."

"Bring me my gun!" called Joel.

"I can't! I'm scared! I'll drop it!" screamed Jinx.

Joel ran to the back steps, keeping his eye on the snake. Beside the banties' chicken pen, there was an old camper, where Dad stored oil and gas cans, paint cans, tools, and other things.

Joel saw the snake go under a board under the chicken pen.
Round the house came the banty hens and rooster. They were
very tame and Rusty crowed loudly. The hawk flew down overhead, making a shadow cross the yard.

"There's gopher hole under there," said Joel. "The snake's
gone under the board to eat gophers."

Jinx stood there screaming, "He'll eat my banties!"

"Be quiet!" cried Joel. "I'll get him. He's a rattler, I'm sure."

Jinx held her hand over her mouth to keep from screaming.

Joel ran in the house to get his gun. As he came out, he
slammed the door and it made a loud bang. Only a minute
before, the hawk had swooped down, grabbed one of the banty
hens and had taken off, flying.

"Oh, my banty! My banty!" cried Jinx, wailing.

The noise of the banging door scared the hawk, who had not too good a hold on the banty. He dropped it to the ground and the little hen ran off cackling. She had had a narrow escape.

Joel stepped out with his gun.

He had to be very careful. The snake was not in sight. Where had it gone? He must make it come out again. He put his gun down. He tipped over to the camper and shook it. With a shovel he poked at the chicken pen and the board under it. The camper fell on the pen and knocked it over. Out came the snake, a big long slithering Pacific rattler.

Joel was ready. He picked up his gun. This was one time he was ready to shoot. He took careful aim and shot. The snake squirmed and lay still. It was all over quickly. Joel breathed a deep breath, although his hand was still shaking.

Just then the banty rooster came around the corner and crowded loudly. Jinx gathered Rusty up in her arms and hugged him tight.

"No snake, no hawk gonna get you, Rusty!" she sobbed.

Joel took his gun in the house. He came out and sat down exhausted.

The yard was a mess. The chicken pen with the baby banties was overturned. Cans of oil and grease had slid out of the camper and been overturned. Oil and grease were everywhere, and worst of all, on the baby chicks.

Jinx stopped crying. She found kerosene and rags and cleaned the chicks off. She put them back in their pen, after Joel set it up again. She fed them and brought them water.

Just then the dogs came tearing up and they all began to bark, as a car drove up the woods road. Mom and Sandy were back from town. They got out of the car and began to unload their packages and bundles.

They had been on a spending spree, all right.

Forgetting all her troubles, Jinx met them and cried out, "What did you buy? What did you buy? Anything for me?"

They carried mysterious packages into the house. Joel and Jinx helped. They began to open them. They showed all the wonderful new things they had bought—six new sweaters, eight new skirts, and a lot of new blouses—all bargains. There was a big new coffee percolator, an automatic toaster, and a whole new set of dishes.

"Wait till you see the new living room set we got!" cried Sandy. "It's coming tomorrow. It was only twenty-five dollars down. A davenport and two big easy chairs."

They had been to Ward's and Penney's and the Roadside Furniture Mart and the discount house. And they went to a show, too. It was all very wonderful.

"I wish I could live in town," said Sandy. "Some day I'll go stay with Aunt Alice in Rogue River. I don't know why I have to stay in the woods all my life."

Joel and Jinx did not listen to her bragging.

"Mom, I'm hungry," said Jinx. "When do we eat? Aint' it time for Dad to be comin' home?"

Mom was so excited over her new purchases, it was hard for her to come down to earth again. Slowly she took off her earrings —they were new, too, and they sparkled—and put on her apron. She looked in the wood-box, but there was no wood to start the fire.

"Joel, Dad told you to get wood in," called Mom.

She took a hard look at the boy. He was a sight, his face and arms streaked with blackberry juice and peanut butter and oil and grease.

"What on earth have you been up to?" Mom asked.

Then she looked at Jinx. The girl was even worse. She looked as if she had been in a battle. All the smudges of jelly and blackberry juice on her face had been streaked with her own tears. And her hair! What was the matter with her hair?

Sandy forgot about Rogue River, as she stared at Jinx. Her eyes opened wide with astonishement.

"Her hair, Mom! Look!" cried Sandy. "It's been cut!"

"Good grief!" cried Mom. "What you kids been up to?"

"I killed a rattler, Mom," said Joel quietly.

"A rattlesnake? Oh, no!" cried Mom, as frightened as Jinx had been a short time before. "Where? How?"

"I shot it with my .22!" said Joel.

"Heck, I don't believe you," said Sandy. "You're just makin' that up."

Joel went out without saying a word. They followed him down the steps. He came back, carrying a stick with the snake looped over it.

"Now, do you believe me, Sandy?" he asked.

"Yes," said Sandy, "but still I don't see . . . "

Mom made Joel cut the head off and bury it. Mom had an idea that a rattler absorbs its poison from the ground, so the head had to be buried. Dad said this notion was all nonsense, but Joel buried the head anyway. He counted the rattles on the tail—there were seven.

Mom started the fire in the stove and put the coffee pot on. She was still feeling good from her trip to town. So she said, "Let's play a trick on Daddy."

Joel and Jinx and Sandy all agreed. It would be fun to fool Dad. All the loggers liked pulling practical jokes.

Out near where Dad parked his pick-up, stood a pile of foundation blocks. They were intended for the new house-to-be. Joel took the snake and Mom helped him coil it in a circle beside the blocks, right where Dad would step out. Then they went back indoors.

"But Jinx's hair!" cried Sandy. "Who cut Jinx's hair?"

Mom hadn't noticed it before. Now as she looked and saw that all of Jinx's long blonde hair had been hacked off. She was shocked.

"You haven't told everything . . ." she began. "I never said you could . . ."

Joel told about the blackberry briars and from the scratches on the children's faces and arms, Mom was forced to believe their story.

"I still don't see why you had to *cut it off!*" cried Mom. "Why didn't you just *pull it out?*"

"I had my knife . . ." Joel began.

"You know, Mom, Joel always has to use that knife," said Sandy. "To keep it sharp, he has to practice with it. It'll cut wood, it'll cut initials in the bark of a tree, it'll open tin cans, it'll cut human hair!"

"Well," said Joel soberly. "What's a knife for, if not to cut?"

They all laughed.

Mom put her arms around Jinx. "You're a sight!" she said.

"It looks better now," said Sandy. "She can see out. Before, she had bangs down to her chin."

Suddenly there was the noise of the pick-up.

"There he is!" cried Joel.

They ran to the door to look out.

Dad stepped out of the truck, reached over to get his lunch bucket, then jumped. He jumped a foot in the air and yelled. He had seen the snake.

"Nellie, bring me my pistol!" he shouted. "Quick! Hurry!"

Mom came out on the step and asked innocently, "What for, honey?"

The question made him pause. He looked first at Mom, then down at the snake. The children crowded around Mom and could no longer keep their faces straight. They began to giggle.

"Great guns!" cried Dad.

He knew he was being taken in.

He gave the snake a good kick and it landed on top of the camper. He looked at the mess of things scattered over the yard. The dogs came up to lick his hands and Rusty the rooster began to crow. When Dad came inside, they told him the whole story. Mom poured him a cup of coffee and everybody talked at once. The snake had seven rattles and Dad was glad Joel had killed it.

Then he saw the stuff Mom had brought back from town.

"What'd you do, buy the whole town out?" he asked.

"No," said Mom, "we left a few things."

Sandy told about the new living-room set and Dad frowned.

"Any of that pay-check left?" he asked.

"Oh, a few pennies!" laughed Mom, shaking her purse.

Then for the first time, Dad's eyes lit on Jinx. She had washed by this time and did not look quite so messy. But her face and arms were still badly scratched, and her hair . . .

Dad pulled her over to him.

"Who cut your hair off, sweetie?" he asked.

"Joel," said Jinx. "He had to, to get me out of the blackberry briars. I got all tangled up."

"Haw, haw, haw!" Dad laughed long and loud.

"Another joke you're playin' on me. O.K. *Haw, haw, haw!"*

He patted her head and let the shaggy short hair fall through his rugged fingers. He gave her a hug and kissed her.

"That's fine," he said. "I need another boy besides Joel. You want to be a logger, too?"

Chapter Four

THE WOODS

ONE day Joel had a chance to go camping with Billy Weber. They planned to camp all night in the woods and return next day. Billy stopped at the Forest Service Station and got a permit.

It was a big job to get ready. The boys took sleeping bags, a frying pan and flashlight. In the packsacks on their backs, they carried bread, peanut cookies, eggs and a chunk of bacon. No drinks—bottles were too heavy. Billy took his rifle along.

Mom offered all kinds of food—sandwiches, cake, bananas, potato chips, wieners, canned beans, and other things.

"This is not a picnic, Mom," said Joel. "We are going camping. We'll kill our own meat and cook it."

Sandy laughed and Mom smiled.

When no one was looking, Joel did put in a can of beans.

"I want to go along," begged Jinx.

"No girls allowed," said Billy Weber.

"But I *want* to go!" cried Jinx. "I can cook for you."

"You're scared of the woods," said Joel. "You're afraid of bears."

So the two boys left without her.

They started up the steep slope behind the house. Once they turned and looked back. There was Jinx sitting on the fence, waving to them. Joel felt sorry for her. He almost wished he had let her come. But still—it was better without girls.

The boys made a beeline for the tall timber, cutting across pastures and slopes covered with brambles and briars. There were fences to climb and piles of brush to scramble over. They huffed and puffed going up the steep grades, then sat down to rest and take it easy for a while. They came to the range where the cows were, and after flapping their arms to scare them, went on. It was a long way to the big woods and they were tired when they got there. They sat down on a log to rest.

How wonderful it was in the forest. Joel and Billy could go where they pleased. Nobody to boss or scold them—what fun it was. No fences they could not climb, no *No Trespassing* signs to hold them back. The forest was a world of green and growing things, a world all its own. Joel took a deep breath.

"We gonna camp here?" he asked.

"Naw," said Billy. "We ain't even near the big woods yet. We got a long ways to go."

He took his compass out of his pocket and studied it. Billy

seemed to know every creek and canyon and trail for miles around, the way he talked.

"First we go to the edge of this canyon, then there's a place we can slide down a piece, and right on that shelf there's a spring . . ." said Billy. "And we can see a hundred miles across the valley. It's purty, but in winter the snow's deep and I don't like it. My feet freeze off."

Overhead a woodpecker was knocking a hole in the side of a tree. The sawdust fell in a shower. A bluejay squawked and a squirrel jumped down and landed at the boys' feet.

Billy reached for his gun.

"What you gonna shoot?" asked Joel.

"That mean old jay," said Billy.

"He's not good to eat," said Joel.

"Naw, but he robs birds' nests and eats their eggs. He's worse'n a crow."

"But we're only gonna shoot to get our food," said Joel.

"I've shot squirrels and rabbits and hawks and crows," bragged Billy. "They're all no good." He put his gun down again.

"Look up there," said Joel.

On the branch of a large pine tree overhead, they saw a little pine squirrel. He jumped from one branch to another. Then, seeing the boys, he began to scold them in his shrill chattering voice. He went back to work, cutting cones off. A shower of cones fell at their feet. The squirrel stopped, cocked his head and listened to the cones hitting the ground.

Joel reached down and picked a cone up. The squirrel came over and barked at him.

"He's sayin', 'Leave my cones alone!' " said Billy, laughing. "He wants to hide them under a wet log to keep them for winter, so he can eat the seeds."

"All right, little fella, you can have them," said Joel.

The boys walked on. The forest was quiet and beautiful with the morning sun slanting through the branches. Off on one side they saw three deer. The deer stood alert for a few minutes, then went leaping away.

"I wish we'd meet an elk," said Billy. "There used to be plenty of them around here. That's how Elk Creek got its name. Old Indian John told my dad he shot the last one."

"There's only deer left now," said Joel.

"But there's plenty of bobcats and cougars," said Billy. "If we look sharp, we might see their tracks."

Billy knew so much about the woods. He showed Joel a bear trail and the hiding place of a fawn. He pointed out a flying squirrel nesting in a woodpecker tree. He told how a bear cub backs down a tree, instead of coming down headfirst. He talked about the way the cougar feed on deer. He saw a tree that had been gnawed by a prickly porcupine. They passed huge rhododendron bushes covered with large pink flowers.

"I've killed a gob of them!" bragged Billy. "Just bop 'em on the nose."

Joel listened with respect and admiration.

The going was rough now. Dead logs and brush lay scattered on the ground. Snags and windfalls blocked the way. The boys had to heave and push branches to get through. Every so often, Billy took out his compass and studied it carefully.

"You sure you know where we're goin'?" asked Joel.

"Yep," said Billy. "We'll get there in half an hour. Just keep a-movin'."

By now Joel had a hard time putting one foot in front of the other. His pack was getting heavier and heavier. But he refused to give up.

At last they came to an open spot, at the bottom of a tree-covered slope. A trickle of water dripped down from the side of the hill under a clump of grass.

"Well, here we are!" cried Billy, breathless and panting.

Joel looked around. There was no open valley, no canyon, no distant view. Trees, trees, nothing but trees on all sides.

"But I thought you said we'd be able to see a hundred miles," said Joel.

"Oh, that was another place," said Billy. "I'll take you there

next time. This spring's O.K. We can camp here."

It was high up all right, but Joel felt a little cheated. He hated to lose faith in Billy, but maybe Billy was just too tired to go on.

Billy flopped down, cupped his hands under the spring water, and lapped it up like a puppy.

"You thirsty?"

Joel took a drink, too.

"My dad calls it 'earth juice,' " Joel said. "Says it's the best drink in the world."

"Better than beer?" asked Billy. *"My* dad says beer's best."

After they rested, the boys built a campfire and got out the frying pan. Billy told Joel to do the cooking. Joel fried bacon, but had a hard time getting an egg into the pan without breaking the yolk. He broke a second one, a banty egg and out fell a little chicken!

The boys laughed.

"Did you bring a settin' egg?" asked Billy. "Leave the chicken in and scramble it."

But Joel dumped it out and started all over again.

While they were eating, Billy heard a noise like footsteps. He walked off to investigate, Joel following. They circled the camp and came back. Nothing. Nobody. Nothing but birds chirping and squawking in the silence.

"You're just hearing things, Billy," said Joel.

They walked around the second time and came back again. They looked at their lunch in dismay. The wrapper was torn off the bread and half the bread was gone. The wrapper on the peanut cookies was broken open, the cookies were broken and scattered. They had not been gone long at all.

"Now what the dickens . . ." cried Billy.

"Somebody's been here," said Joel. "Whoever you heard walking in the woods sneaked in here and stole our food."

"Looks that way," said Billy.

Usually Billy had all the answers, but this time he was stumped.

The boys cleared up their lunch, put out their fire and doused it, then went exploring. Billy led the way to Old Indian John's cabin. It had fallen to pieces and was now only a pile of logs. The ground was packed hard around it and Billy found tracks.

"A cougar's been here," he said, looking closely. "It's been stalking two deer."

Joel shook with fear. "Sure it's not a bear track or a bobcat?"

"It's a cougar for sure," said Billy. "Gee! Wouldn't I like to meet him!"

"Oh no!" cried Joel.

"What? You spooked?" asked Billy. "He's just a great big old pussycat. He's scared of people. He'll run away if he sees you. All he wants is a big fat deer for his dinner."

"A bobcat is bad enough," said Joel. "Could you shoot a bobcat with your .22, Billy?"

"You got to have a cat-dog," said Billy, "trained just to run bobcats, and you got to do it at night. After twenty minutes, the bobcat's trail gets cold, so he's hard to get."

Billy's father, though a logger, liked to lay off work frequently and spend his time hunting and fishing. Billy had learned a lot from his dad.

"Soon as I'm thirteen, I'm gonna get a deer license," said Billy.

"I'll hunt 'em with a big rifle. Ketch one grazing, sneak up across a log-pile, and wham! I got him. Then put my tag on him!"

"And have good venison to eat!" added Joel. "Golly! *Is* it good! Wish I had a hunk right now."

"Once a big chicken hawk was after our chickens," said Billy. "I took Dad's double-barreled shotgun and tried to shoot it. I was just a little kid then. The gun was so heavy, I had a hard time holding it up. I shot, but all it did was knock me flat on my fanny!"

Joel laughed with Billy.

The boys came back to their camp and Joel started the fire up again. The twigs were damp and it began to smoke badly.

"I hear something," cried Joel, suddenly. "Footsteps."

"Somebody's coming," said Billy. "I hear it, too. Heck, why can't they leave us alone?"

He tried to look unconcerned, but Joel could see he was nervous.

"It might be the Forest Service guy," said Billy. "Hide your matches."

They waited and soon a young man came up, whistling. Billy was right. He wore the green Forest Service uniform, with a shoulder patch on his sleeve and a badge on his pocket.

"Hi, boys!" he said in a friendly voice. "You campin' out?"

"Yes," said Billy, crossly. "Gonna sleep here tonight."

"That's fine," said the man. "My name's Bob Downey. You can call me Bob. I saw the smoke from your campfire and I thought I'd better come over."

"We got a permit," said Billy.

"Good!" said Bob.

He sat down on a log and Joel brought him a drink of spring water.

"I'm making a survey of bug-killed trees in this area," he said.

Billy was still angry.

"What d'you mean stealin' our bread and cookies?" he demanded. "If you'd a asked us, we'd a give you some. If you was that hungry . . ."

Bob Downey laughed.

"I didn't steal any of your food," he said.

"Yes you did, we heard you," said Billy. "We heard footsteps off a ways and we walked out and all around to investigate, and when we come back, half our bread was gone and a lot of cookies."

"Your camp was robbed?" asked Bob.

"It sure was," said Joel.

"No animal tracks?" asked Bob.

"Not one," said Billy. "I looked."

"There's another robber you overlooked," said Bob, "and he doesn't leave tracks. He's called Clark's nutcracker—but his common name is *Camp Robber*."

"You mean a bird?" asked Billy.

"Yes," said Bob. "He's pretty as all get out, big as a bluejay, gray all over, black and white on his wings, and a bright red spot on his black beak. He's so tame, he's not afraid of anything or anybody."

"I've seen him," said Billy, "but I didn't know . . ."

"You turn your back," said Bob, "and he'll come up and get into everything that's loose, lookin' for food. He'll even eat cooked pan potatoes and raw meat!"

"I never knew that," said Billy.

The boys laughed. It was Billy's turn to learn something new. Then he grew suspicious again.

"But the bread and cookies were sealed up tight in wrappers," he said.

"Paper won't stop a nutcracker," said Bob, laughing. "He gives it a few pecks and tears it to pieces."

"Won't you sample the remains?" said Joel, offering cookies.

"These are swell," said Bob. "No wonder old Camp Robber enjoyed them."

Before he left, the Forest Service man warned the boys about their campfire.

"You don't need to tell us all that Smokey Bear stuff!" growled Billy. "We know all that. Our dads are loggers."

"Well," said Bob, "even loggers have to watch out. There's one good rule. Be careful with matches, and make double sure you've put your campfire out. Douse it good!"

"As if we don't know that!" muttered Billy.

After the man left, the boys sat a while by their campfire, talking. Once they saw a flash of white overhead as a flying squirrel sailed by. Night came, they doused their fire and crawled into their sleeping bags. They talked a while, watching the moonlight through the branches of the great fir trees, and then began to get sleepy.

Joel was happy. This was the life! Better than staying at home and sleeping indoors. All those jobs to do at home—slop the pigs, pick off potatoe bugs in the garden, chop firewood and bring it in. Up here on the mountain, nothing to do but enjoy life, watch the animals, eat when you feel like it and sleep when you get tired.

He loved all the woods animals—the chipmunks and squirrels, the porcupines, the rabbits, the skunks and the weasels, the deer, the beavers, the gophers and the raccoons . . . He even loved the bobcats, the bears, and the cougars, though he did not see them often. He began to doze . . . At home, just barking dogs and meowing cats, crowing banties and stupid cows and pokey old horses. No fun with them. He dozed again. There were crows and hawks and bluejays and owls . . .

Suddenly he raised up, wide awake. He heard a noise. Something was moving. Some kind of animal was walking around.

"Billy!" he whispered softly, poking him in the ribs.

Billy woke at once and said, "What is it?"

"I hear an animal walking in the grass."

"Aw, gwan," said Billy. "Go back to sleep."

Joel lay down again. Again he heard the noise. Now it was close to his head. He reached for his flashlight and flashed it on the clump of grass beside him. Two big frogs jumped out.

Joel chuckled. Nothing but frogs! Good thing Billy was asleep again.

He tried to go to sleep, but couldn't. The woods were full of night noises—chirps and rattlings and rustlings and bustlings. Were all the birds and animals up and wide awake? Did they never sleep? He heard some squeaks and squeals. What was that? Mice, gophers, chipmunks? Then suddenly a loud screech. He jumped nervously. A long *too-whoo-oooo* came at intervals. Oh, yes, that was an owl.

The owls were spooky things, they could see at night. They lived in holes in hollow trees. They slept in the daytime and flew around at night. There were all kinds—the great-horned owl, the little bitty pigmy owl, the barn owl, the cat-faced owl. Dad had shown him one once, that looked just like a cat. To Joel they were all screech owls, because they screeched so loudly. *Too-whoo-oooo! Too-whoo-oooo!* he heard it again. They preyed on little animals at night—mice and small rabbits, all kinds of birds, grouse and quail and even turkey. A loud shriek, then a whish and a bump!

That's an owl and he's caught his prey. Joel told himself. It was their way of life. They had to eat. They liked the night the way people liked daylight. Old Mother Nature had things worked out pretty well. She made the big woods to shelter and provide food for all the animals. Even the big animals, too—the bear, the deer, the cougar. The forest was their home. Here

they found food and shelter and here they raised their young.

Joel had never thought much about these things before. He seemed to understand them better now. As he lay awake in the moonlight, he felt happier than he had been in a long time.

Another loud screech and a big bump. This time Joel wasn't scared at all. He heard more chirpings and chatterings. What was going on? What did all the birds and squirrels and other animals do when no people were around? Play? Have fun? Throw pine cones at each other? Or just gather their food and eat?

Joel felt almost like a pine squirrel himself. *The seeds in the cones of the sugar pine are good,* he said to himself. *They taste like nuts. It must be fun to be a squirrel . . . until a man comes with a gun.*

He dozed and fell asleep.

For breakfast next morning, Joel fried the rest of the eggs and the last of the bacon. The boys finished the bread and cookies.

"I'm still hungry," said Joel, after they ate.

"I'll go out and shoot some game," said Billy, "a squirrel or a rabbit, maybe. Or a bird of some kind."

"How do I cook it?" asked Joel.

"Wait till I get it," said Billy. "If it's grouse, we'll cut it up and put the pieces on a stick and brown 'em in the fire. Get a bed of coals ready."

Joel stayed at camp and waited. After he washed out the frying pan, there was nothing to do. He heard a shot and soon Billy came back, emptyhanded.

"Get a squirrel?" he asked.

"No," said Billy. "They're not fit to eat anyhow."

"I heard a shot," said Joel. "Did you miss?"

"No, got a chipmunk," said Billy.

"Oh, no!" cried Joel in dismay.

"Looky here!" Billy had three baby chipmunks inside his shirt. "They were in the hollow of a snag over there."

"You shot the mother?" cried Joel.

"Sure," said Billy. "She was scoldin' me and runnin' at me, as if she wanted to scratch my eyes out!"

"She wouldn't hurt you, you know that," said Joel. "She was just protecting her babies. Now they'll die."

"No they won't," said Billy. "Take 'em home with you."

It was better than leaving them to die in the woods. Joel made a nest of leaves in the lunch box and put the chipmunks in. Since Billy brought no game, there was no cooking to be done. Joel brought out his emergency can of beans, pried the top off with his knife and the boys ate cold beans. Then they broke camp and started for home.

Along the way, they came to a huge Douglas fir tree. All the trees in the area were large, but this was the largest. The boys stood at the base and looked up. The trunk went up and up and at the top it was crowned with a circle of branches against the blue sky.

"Bet this is larger than that giant sugar pine on Jackson Creek," said Billy, "and bigger even than that tallest cedar at Tiller." He stretched his arms out wide. "It's more'n six feet in diameter and over two hundred feet high. Bet there's enough wood in this one tree to build three big houses!"

Joel agreed.

"How would you like to be a high-climber and top it?" Billy asked.

"Not me," said Joel, "but I bet my dad could. Dad says it's a challenge to put on his spurs and go climbin' up, choppin' off the side branches and flipping his rope. And after he has sawed off the top and watched it fall, he gets a free ride. The tree swings back and forth as much as fifteen feet!"

"But he don't do that every day," said Billy, "and not on big trees like this."

"No," said Joel. "The Forest Service is savin' these giants. They never mark them for cutting. Dad goes to a new location where they need a spar-pole, and a spar-pole's got to be plenty big to hold all those cables. My dad's not afraid of anything. Most men don't like to top a tree, but my dad does."

"It tears a man up," said Billy. "That's why they don't like to do it. They can get killed easy."

"Most of the time Dad falls smaller trees," said Joel. "Dad's a faller and a bucker, a choker-setter, a powder-monkey, a hooker, a shovel-operator—and he's good at all of them."

Billy hiked on ahead, feeling jealous. His own dad was lazy and tried to get out of work when he could.

"Your dad'll get *his* one of these days," predicted Billy. "Every logger that ever lived has got most of his bones broken. He'll get *his!*"

"What d'you mean?" asked Joel. "A logger don't go till his time comes. Dad's had plenty accidents. He's had four concussions, three broken ribs, and five broken noses!"

Billy said nothing more and the boys walked on in silence.

How proud Joel was of Dad, and how lucky Dad was to spend his life out in the woods. Out in the open air, in the warm sun, using his muscles, his strong arms and legs, but his head, too! If you didn't use your head in the woods, you'd get into trouble. What fun to climb a tree a hundred and fifty feet high and sway up there in the wind! Free and independent—nobody to boss him around. Afraid? Of course not. He was not afraid of the big trees, or the big logs or the big machines. Dad could do anything. He was calm as a toad, quick as a cat, fierce as a cougar, and strong as a horse.

Joel made up his mind. Some day he'd be a logger like Dad, in stagged pants, calk boots, and tin hat. He could hardly wait to grow up.

Chapter Five

THE PRIZE

"JINX! Jinx!" called Joel. "What are you doing?"

Jinx was standing by her rooster pen. She had a black cloth over the top. The rooster was inside. Beside her on the ground were two old wastepaper baskets and a flowered lamp shade.

Joel came over to see. "What on earth . . .?"

Jinx threw a handful of grain into the pen, then grabbed the black cloth off the top.

"Now crow, Rusty! Crow!" she cried.

The rooster obliged. He crowed lustily, then ate the grain.

"I'm teaching him to crow," said Jinx. "I'm going to enter him at the Rooster Crow Contest at Rogue River next week. Aunt Alice wrote about it and asked us to come and bring our roosters. If I can win First Prize, I'll get one hundred and fifty dollars!"

"Wow!" said Joel.

"But he has to crow steadily for half an hour," said Jinx.

She covered the pen again with the black cloth.

"Look what I brought," said Joel. "Billy found 'em up on the mountain when we were camping."

Jinx looked in the lunch box and saw the three baby chipmunks.

"Give 'em to me," she said. "I'll tame 'em."

"Wait a minute," said Joel. "Go get a small carton. Let's make a nest for them."

"I'll name 'em," said Jinx. "How about Chip, Chap, and Chum?"

"That's fine," said Joel.

They took stuffing out of an old mattress and lined the carton. Then Joel got his old coonskin cap and put it in one corner.

"I'll put the tail up," he said, "so they'll think it's their mother."

Jinx fed the chipmunks soft oatmeal and milk-soaked bread. She put the box behind the stove, where it would be undisturbed. Mom said it was O.K.

The chipmunks grew fast. Soon they could eat other things— lettuce and carrots, peanuts and sunflower seed. They liked bread and would even nibble fruitcake. In a few days they climbed out of the box and had the run of the house.

Gypsy, the house-cat, was banished. She had to stay outside. The three dogs, as much at home inside as outside, paid no attention to the new pets.

One day, when Jinx was training her rooster, she saw Gypsy go by with something in her mouth.

"You villain, you!" she cried. "What have you got?"

It was not a mouse. It was Chip, one of the pet chipmunks. Jinx chased the house-cat away and took poor Chip inside. She put Vicks salve on the spot where the cat had bit it. She put Chip down.

"You can pick him up, Joel," said Jinx. "He's real tame. He won't hurt you, honest."

Joel picked the chipmunk up and it bit him. He dropped it quickly.

"Get me some iodine!" he yelled.

Mom swabbed the bite and put a Band-Aid on.

"He's *not* tame," said Joel to Jinx. "Chipmunks are wild. Let's let 'em go back to the woods. You can't tame them."

"I bet I can," said Jinx.

Mom didn't like it much, the way the chipmunks had the run of the house. She never knew when or where one would pop out. Chip lived in the dish cupboard and whenever she reached for a dish, there he was. Chap liked the cushions on the davenport, so people often sat on him. But the littlest one, Chum, lived in the pocket of Big Joe's old overalls, hanging on a nail. Chum chewed a hole in the pocket, from which he could look out and see what was going on.

One day at noon, Mom got all dressed up in her best clothes. Dot Kramer came in her car and they drove off. They did not say where they were going.

Joel stretched out on the new davenport. The three dogs

jumped up to keep him company. A tussle began. The dogs
barked, Joel poked and pounded them, pushing them off, but
they just jumped back up again.

"Oh, Joel!" cried Sandy. "On our new davenport! Those dogs
are full of loose hairs and they've been in the creek, their paws
are muddy!"

Sandy had washed her hair and was putting it up in rollers.

All of a sudden, Dad walked in. It was early afternoon and
nobody was expecting him. His face was unshaven and dirty, his
overalls were sticky with pitch. He stomped his calk boots as he
went to the washbasin in the corner of the kitchen. He set his
lunch box down and threw his tin hat on the floor.

"What's cookin'?" he asked.

"Nothin'," said Joel. "Mom's gone away."

Big Joe sloshed water over his face and arms. He took off his shirt and washed his chest and back. He got out his razor and shaved. All this time he said nothing.

What was it? Something wrong? Why was Dad home so early?

Joel sat up on the davenport and tried to make the dogs behave. They thought it was just a game, so they kept on yapping and growling. They jumped up and licked Joel's face.

Jinx ran tearing through the house, chasing one of the chipmunks. Sandy ran after her, screaming, "Mom said for me to wash your hair! You'd better come before I clobber you!"

Dad looked around. He was big all right, that's why he was called Big Joe. Joel wondered if he'd ever grow as big as Dad, or as strong. Just look at those muscles and all that hair on his chest. No sissy could be a logger, he knew that.

"Where's Mom?" asked Dad.

"I don't know," said Joel. "She went off somewhere with Dot Kramer in Dot's car. She didn't say where she was goin'."

"Get off that davenport, you and those dirty dogs!" shouted Dad.

Joel jumped as if he'd been shot. He grabbed the dogs by their collars and tried to pull them off. They liked the davenport as much as he did. They refused to budge. He had to pummel them to get off, and drag them out the door by sheer force.

"Jinx! Sandy!" called Dad.

The girls came running.

"Get to work here! Clean up this pigpen! Look at all the rubbish!"

He pointed to the corners of the room, where all sorts of things were lying—old cans and bottles, dirty clothing and shoes, tools and wastepaper, magazines, candy wrappers, and empty cartons.

"Get a broom! Get a scrubbing mop! Clean this place up."

He pointed to the davenport and the two big arm chairs.

"A month ago they were NEW!" shouted Dad. "Two payments made on them and they're shot already."

Jinx and Sandy, shamefaced, set to work.

Dad cleared old shoes, newspapers, and apple parings off one of the big armchairs and sat down in it with a thump. He turned the TV on and a terrifying noise filled the room. Joel came back inside. He helped to clean up the rubbish.

"Where does this go?" he asked, holding up one object after the other.

Sandy told him where to put things.

Jinx came over and whispered to Joel: "I bet Dad's been fired. That's why he's so mad."

"No," whispered Joel. "He's too good a worker. The boss wouldn't fire him. He's mad because he's hungry and Mom's not here and dinner's not ready."

Big Joe heard the children whispering.

"Get to work there! I'm fed up with the lot of you!"

He shouted above the TV din, loud enough so the children could not fail to hear.

In no time at all, the house looked better. Joel and Jinx slipped outside, and Sandy soon followed.

"He fell asleep in his chair," said Sandy. "He's just tired, that's all."

They stayed outside until after Mom came back. She was dressed in her newest nylon jersey dress and had her shiniest earrings on. Her spike heels clicked up the back steps as she went in at the door. She did not say where she had been or what she had been doing.

The children let Mom go in alone. They gave her no warning. Then they waited. They expected to hear some kind of explosion, but none came. They heard voices and a little later, they smelled food cooking. Some time later, Mom called them in to supper. She had fried chicken to eat and it was good.

"You got home early, Joe?" asked Mom, sweetly.

"Yes," said Dad. "Ordered off work. Humidity down to twenty today. There's sure to be a forest fire if this keeps up."

No wonder Dad was worried.

The Rooster Crow Contest was held the week before the Fourth of July. It was an all-day affair. It began at ten in the morning with a parade, and the contest was held at three in the afternoon.

On the way over Sandy rode in the front seat of the old Ford with Mom, while Jinx and Joel rode in the back, with Rusty in his cage between them. Joel did not want to go at all—he just went along to help Jinx. It took about an hour to get to Rogue River, and they were late in getting started. Rusty crowed lustily all the way, so Jinx was happy. All her training had not been for nothing.

When they got there, the town was crowded with people. The parade had started, so Mom found a parking place and they hurried over. All but Jinx who refused to leave Rusty.

"Somebody might steal him!" she said. "And if we close up the car, he'll have a heatstroke. I've got to find water for him to drink."

After the parade, Mom drove to Aunt Alice's, where they had lunch. Everybody admired Rusty's cage. Jinx had made it from two wicker wastebaskets, one upturned over the other, with the flowered and ruffled lampshade on top. Jinx took Rusty out of his cage and the little cousins, Bobby and Ronnie, clapped their hands when he crowed. At last they started for the school yard. Jinx and Joel carried Rusty in his cage, and the others trailed along behind.

Joel began to wish he had never come. There were too many people, and worse still, too many roosters. Everybody else had the same idea—of training a rooster to win a prize. Boys and girls of all ages and sizes were bringing in all kinds of outlandish cages, with roosters of all sizes, shapes, and colors. There were poor old scroungy ones and big fat Plymouth Rocks. And plenty of banties, plenty of Golden Seabrights just like Rusty. In fact there were more banties than any other kind. Everybody seemed to think like Jinx, that banties crowed the most and the loudest. In a mob like this, how could poor little old Rusty win a prize?

Joel and Jinx stared at all the fancy cages. A price offered for the most original cage had brought out some fearful concoctions —pens made like igloos and medieval castles, tepees and Quonset huts; pens made out of hardware cloth, dish drainers, sifters, and sieves, or just plain chicken wire; cages trimmed with flowers and foliage and tissue paper and ribbon bows. There were as many kinds as there were owners. On the cages were labels with the roosters' names in large letters: Dandy, Gold Nugget, Black

Fella, Casey, Sugarfoot, Eureka, Golden Feathers, and others.

All around were people milling, men in cowboy boots and hats, women in flowered dresses, younger ones in pants, little boys riding ponies, young mothers pushing babies in carriages, children hanging onto balloons and letting them go. It was dusty and hot in the open schoolyard, but nobody seemed to mind, as they wandered among the concession booths and exhibits, and looked over the rooster cages.

"Too many people!" growled Joel. "I don't like this."

"Aw, come on," said Jinx. "Let's find a place."

They had to register the rooster, then find a place for him on one of the tables under the row of shade trees. At last they squeezed Rusty's cage in between two others. Crowing Oscar was on one side and Little Moe on the other. Crowing Oscar was

a white leghorn and Little Moe a banty. The girl who owned Crowing Oscar said she had been crowing back at him for a week. The boy who owned Little Moe said Moe was an orphan, one of four, Eeenie, Meenie, Minie and Moe. The other three had died.

"He's tame," said the boy. "He's used to people."

All the noise and conversation and excitement and crowing came to a sudden halt, when at 3 P.M a policeman fired a blank cartridge to start the "Crow." All the owners had been moved down six places, to stand before someone else's cage, to keep tally. Each person had pencil and pad to make a mark each time the rooster in front of him crowed. The rooster who crowed most often in half an hour was to win the prize.

Everybody was excited, even the roosters.

Joel was in the line for counting, so Jinx stayed as near Rusty as possible. When she heard the shot, she pulled off the black cloth, but Rusty did not respond.

"Crow, Rusty, crow!" cried Jinx. She clapped her hands, she blew in his face, she scattered his feed. But Rusty did not crow.

A man leaned over the rope behind her, which kept spectators back.

"Wring his neck!" he said. "Make chicken dumplings out of him and eat him tomorrow."

Jinx turned around and glared. She was madder at the man than at Rusty. Just then Rusty crowed. Jinx clapped her hands. Rusty's attendant marked down one crow.

Jinx noticed the other roosters and listened to comments.

"That one just eats."

"Golden Feathers hasn't crowed once."

"Champ looks sick. He's moulting."

"Big Mouth keeps it shut. He'll keep everybody awake all night."

The other contestants were having troubles, too. But now that Rusty had started, he kept on, so Jinx was hopeful.

A man in a big white Stetson hat marked KSHA Radio kept coming around and making announcements through a microphone.

"Anybody over 20 crows?" "In third place right now is 26 crows." "Independence has 32, Black Fella—35, Little Baldy—40 . . . Ah! We're goin' up now. Rusty—51, and 65 for Matchstick . . . Let's beat the record of 109 crows in 1953! Keep crowin', all you little roosters and win that prize!"

Then all at once it was over. Another shot rang out, a giant voice over the loudspeaker announced that the First Prize winner had crowed 95 times in half an hour, Second Prize, 80 times, Third Prize, 69 times.

Joel hurried back to Jinx.

"Who got it? Who got it?" he asked. "Did you hear the names?"

"No," said Jinx. "Rusty did pretty good, but . . ."

The next minute somebody grabbed Rusty in his cage and somebody else took Jinx by the arms and marched off with her. Joel had to hurry to keep up. Where were they going? Where were Mom and Sandy and Aunt Alice and her family? He couldn't see them in the crowd anywhere.

Then, up on the platform, whom should he see but Jinx. Other boys and girls stood beside her in a row. The loudspeaker was

shouting and people were clapping. But Rusty—Rusty had not
crowed enough. Something was wrong somewhere. Somebody
had made a mistake. Why didn't Jinx tell them?

Joel looked around. People were crowded around the grandstand. There at the back he saw Mom and Sandy and Aunt
Alice and the boys. They were all clapping hard. On the platform
now, Jinx was standing at the microphone. The man beside
her announced:

"This little girl, Jinx Bartlett, came all the way from Drum to
enter her rooster Rusty. Rusty didn't quite make First Prize, but
Jinx gets ten dollars for having entered from the farthest distance,"—he handed her an envelope—"and ten dollars more for
the best decorated cage!"—then another envelope. The crowd
clapped noisily.

Joel heard Jinx say in a high clear voice, "Thank you very much. Next year my rooster will do better."

The crowd clapped again, still louder.

Then it was all over and the people got down from the grandstand. First Prize, 95 crows went to Matchstick, Second Prize, 80 crows to Black Fella, and Third Prize, 69 crows to Jasper. Even though Rusty did not crow enough, Jinx was happy. She grinned from ear to ear.

"Good grief!" cried Mom, when they pushed their way through the crowd and finally located Jinx with Rusty in his cage. "If I'd a known you were winning a prize, I'd a washed your hair and got you a new dress."

"Too late now," said Joel.

"She looks like a gypsy," said Aunt Alice, "with all that ragged hair."

"It's a 'pixie' haircut," said Sandy, "the homemade kind!"

Jinx put her prize money in Mom's purse and Joel helped her carry Rusty in his cage to the car.

The Rooster Crow was over for another year.

Excitements seemed to come in bunches. Right after the Rooster Crow came the Fourth of July.

"Let's have a picnic," Sandy and Jinx begged Mom. "Everybody has a picnic on the Fourth of July."

"Your Dad hates picnics," said Mom. "Remember he has a picnic lunch every day in the woods. It's no fun for him."

"At least we'll have a snowball fight," said Jinx.

From the freezer she took out a dozen snowballs she had

saved from last winter. They had frozen into balls of ice. She and Joel threw them at each other.

Then Dot Kramer came and said that an old-fashioned loggers' picnic was being held at Jed Allen's place, and everybody was invited. Mom and the girls got ready to go. Joel said he wouldn't go unless Dad did. When he saw Dad putting on clean jeans and shirt, and shaving, Joel got ready, too. He figured Billy Weber would be there and maybe Jim Hunter and Snuff Carter and some of the other boys.

The picnic was a great letdown, at least for Joel—all but the food, which wasn't half bad.

Joel went in at the kitchen door. The Allens' kitchen was a madhouse. It was jammed with men and women, shouting, laughing, joking, drinking, and pounding each other on the back. Joel squeezed through into the living room. Here, all the furniture had been pushed back against the wall and people were sitting there watching. In the center of the floor dancing was going on, to the tune of two noisy guitars played by two men from the local tavern, over in the corner.

Children of all ages ran in and out, bumping into the dancers and being stepped on, crying and having to be picked up, and eating and dropping cookie crumbs, and spilling ice cream and yelling. Most of the dancers were loggers, who danced with the same vigor that made them loggers, throwing their partners around with wild abandon. The women sometimes got winded and had to sit down to catch their breath before they got up and went at it again.

Gosh! thought Joel. *And they call this a picnic!* It was hot and stuffy in the small room and smelly from perspiration of the hard-working dancers who thought they were having fun. Young people were not dancing, only the middle-aged and old. Crying babies and loggers—what a combination!

Joel stomped out the door.

In the field beside the house, he could at least breathe clean air. He saw Snuff and Jim and went over to join them. Billy Weber was there, too. They had been turning cartwheels. It was fun for a while, then they wondered about the food.

"The women were fixing salads in the kitchen as I came through," said Joel.

"And the barbecued chicken is ready," said Billy. "Ed Adkins said he'd cooked twelve chickens. Let's go eat."

At the back of the house, tables had been set up in the grass.

Two women were bringing food out. Besides fried chicken, they brought wieners, potato chips, potato salad, baked beans, and buns. The boys found paper plates and began to fill them. They sat on the ground and ate.

"What! No desserts?" cried Billy Weber.

How funny. There were no puddings, pies, or cakes. Not even Jell-O. The men and women, drinking and dancing inside the house, did not come out to eat. The noisy twang of the guitars, the laughing and shouting kept on and on. Would it go on all night and the next day, too?

Joel did not see Mom and Dot Kramer at all. Where were they—inside somewhere? Jinx and Sandy and the Kramer girls, Donna and Sherry, found plates and filled them. Dad and Jake Hunter and Harry Carter and a couple of other men squatted on their haunches at the side of the house. Joel filled a plate high and gave it to Dad. Dad took it and began to eat. But he never stopped talking.

Joel sat down beside the men to listen.

What were they talking about?

Logging, of course. They were logging in words, not in deeds. They were cat-logging and high-leading and truck-driving. They were listening to whistle signals and watching out for guy lines and dodging chokers. They were enjoying broken ribs and sprained ankles and brain concussions. They were fearless and unafraid, never tired, always brave.

It was good talk to listen to.

Joel was glad he had come to the picnic, after all.

Chapter Six

THE RUNAWAY

THE vegetable garden was halfway up the hill. It was planted to vegetables—beans, tomatoes, carrots, beets, but mostly potatoes. There were endless rows of potatoes, because Mom wanted enough to last all winter. And the potatoes were full of potato bugs.

Something had to be done about it, so Dad told the children to pick potato bugs. They could not go swimming until the vines were clean. Dad meant what he said. There were four rows of potatoes for Sandy, four for Joel, and four for Jinx. All morning, Sandy and Joel worked hard, stopping only now and then to straighten their backs. They carried small cans of kerosene and knocked the bugs off into the cans. They came back after lunch to finish up.

But Jinx would not help.

She had many excuses. Her banties, her baby chicks, her chipmunks needed her attention. Her head ached, her back ached, her legs ached. The sun might give her sunstroke. The truth was she did not like to pick potato bugs and was trying to get out of it. But nobody took pity on her, or offered to do her job for her.

Joel and Sandy finished their job and went away.

"*We're* going swimming!" they cried. "You can't go till you do your job."

They put on their bathing suits and ran down the woods road.

"I'm coming with you," called Jinx.

"Better get after those potato bugs first," warned Joel.

Jinx felt sorry for herself. Now she was left alone to do a hateful job. Why did they have to go away and leave her? Why did Dad choose such hateful jobs for his kids to do? Now Mom was easy. If you made a fuss about doing something, Mom would usually end up by doing it herself. But not Dad. Dad was strict. What Dad said, had to be done, or there would be trouble.

Slowly she went back up the hill to the garden. The sun was hot now, hotter than it had been all morning. She got her can of kerosene and went into the potato patch. She began picking the potato bugs off one by one, flipping them into the kerosene.

What was the use of having a garden anyhow? Something always ate up the vegetables—rabbits or deer or porcupines of bugs or worms. Or else they dried up in midsummer, if you didn't water them. Why not let the potato bugs eat the potato vines? Poor things! They needed some food to eat! And that would save all the trouble of digging the potatoes in the fall.

Jinx knocked a bug into her can and sighed. Suddenly she felt someone was watching her. She looked up. There was Billy Weber.

He scowled, staring at her.

"What 'ja doin'?" he asked.

"Pickin' potato bugs. Wanna help?"

"Naw!" said Billy.

He just stood there and stared.

"What you want?" asked Jinx.

"Nothin'," said Billy.

Jinx shoved some more bugs into her can. She did not like to be watched. She wished Billy would go away. But he didn't. He just kept on standing there.

"Does your mother know you're over here?" asked Jinx.

"Naw," said Billy. "Never tell her where I'm goin'."

"Won't you catch it when you get home?" asked Jinx.

"Naw," said Billy. Then he added. "A lickin' don't last long and a scoldin' don't hurt."

Jinx had to laugh. It was true.

"Where's Joel?" asked Billy.

"Gone swimmin' with Sandy," said Jinx. "Down in the creek, back of the store."

Billy turned and left. He walked slowly down the woods road. He would be going swimming, too, right in his clothes. He did not have any bathing trunks.

The other kids were all swimming there now, too. The Kramer girls and Betty Carter would be there, maybe others. Everybody but Jinx. She felt very sorry for herself. She looked at the long rows of potato plants. They looked endless. It would take *years* to get to the end . . . Besides, she hated picking potato bugs.

Jinx set the can down in the middle of the row. This was the limit. She refused to pick another bug. But what would Dad say when he came home at night? She knew she could not face him. She did not want a licking or even a bawling out.

"I'll show them!" she said aloud. "I'll just run away!"

The idea was a good one. Immediately she felt better. This was an idea that meant action—not just squatting in a potato patch in the hot sun.

She ran into the house.

Good thing Mom was gone for the day with Dot Kramer, so the coast was clear. She ran to her bedroom, found a battered old suitcase and threw her clothes into it. She borrowed Sandy's comb and brush and also a string of pretty beads from Mom's bureau. She found her purse with her money and tucked that in, too. No telling how much she might need—in a strange location.

It would be fun to live somewhere else for a while. Then they would all be sorry. Jinx snapped her suitcase shut, full of excitement and determination. She wrote a little note and set it up on the kitchen table.

"I'm running away from home," it said. "Don't try to find me." She signed it *Jinx*.

"Oh yes, a little food," she cried, stopping at the icebox. "No telling when or where I'll get my next meal."

She picked up a small box of cornflakes, some cookies, and a banana. Then she took time to make two cheese sandwiches. She put the food into a paper sack and tucked it inside the suitcase. It was enough to take care of an emergency.

She marched off down the woods road, swinging her suitcase at her side. Somehow it was very exciting to be running away. Why had she never thought of it before? Too bad there wasn't someone to see her go. But no, it was better if they didn't. That would spoil it all.

When she reached the highway, she could hear the boys and girls in the swimming hole. They were yelling and screaming and she knew they were having fun. She wished she could join them. For a moment, she thought of hiding her suitcase under a bush and going over to have a swim.

But awkward questions—about potato bugs—would be asked. No, it was better to stick to her plan. Jinx was not one to be easily diverted. She was running away and so run she must.

She started south on the highway, walking along in the weeds and grass at one side of the road. She walked as fast as she could go. She hoped no one that she knew would pass by and stop to ask questions. An awful thought crossed her mind. What if Mom and Dot Kramer came along in Dot's car and saw her? No. There was no danger. They would not be back for hours yet.

She kept on walking . . .

Joel did not enjoy his swim very much. The water felt cold and made his teeth chatter. Goose pimples came over his arms

and legs. He sat on a rock in the sun to try to get warm. Billy
came and sat beside him. They talked about cat-logging.

Then the girls started splashing water on them. Donna
Kramer picked up crawdads and threw them. Sherry teased Joel
and said his hair was turning green from the creek water. Sandy
and Sherry began fighting over a towel. Sandy knocked Sherry's
glasses off into the water. The girls began quarreling, each
blaming the other. Sherry made Sandy and Donna and Betty
wade in the creek, hunting for her glasses.

Joel wondered why Jinx did not come. She must be through
bug-picking by this time. She liked swimming more than anyone
else. She was slow—she hated that job. Maybe he'd better go
help her.

Billy Weber was bored with the girls and got up to go. So Joel
left, too.

Yes, he'd go help Jinx, so she could be done with her job before Dad got home. Then nobody would get bawled out.

Joel ran up the woods road and on up the hill to the vegetable garden. But Jinx was not there. He looked at her rows of potatoes. They were still full of potato bugs. There sat her can of kerosene in the path.

"Jinx! J—i—n—x!" called Joel.

She must have gone back to the house. Joel ran indoors, calling her name. No answer. No one there. The house was forlorn and empty.

Then he saw it—the paper on the kitchen table.

He picked it up and read the words:

"I'm running away from home. Don't try to find me. Jinx."

Joel frowned. Jinx running away? Jinx always so cheerful and happy, why was she running away?

Joel went in her room. The closet door was open and he saw that her clothes were gone, but not Sandy's. This was more serious than he thought. Did she really mean it? Would Jinx really run away from home?

Joel took off his bathing trunks and put on his pants and shirt. He looked at the paper again, and read it over and over. It sounded final, as if she really meant it. But where would she go? Where does anybody go, when they run away from home?

One thing was sure, Joel would have to find her. He would find her right away and bring her back. He crumpled her note in a wad and stuffed it into his pants pocket. He ran down the woods road. When he got to the highway, he stopped. Which way should he go?

To the store, first, of course.

Myra might know something.

But Myra didn't.

"Where's Jinx?" Joel asked. "Have you seen her?"

"No," said Myra, looking up from her book. "Why? She lost?"

Now how did Myra guess?

Joel shook his head.

"You sure you ain't seen her?" he asked again. "She's not hidin' in back somewhere?"

"Go and look," said Myra.

Joel went all through the store and the little post office, but Jinx was not there.

"I don't hide kids," said Myra. "Last time I saw Jinx was yesterday when I gave her your mail."

Joel had to believe her.

He went out the door and stood by the gas tanks uncertainly. Which way should he go? To the south, on the road to Medford, or to the north on the canyon road to River Bend and Canyonville? Where would a girl go when she was running away from home?

Just then a Chevvy drove up from the south. It stopped by the store and the driver sounded his horn. He was a stranger, Joel had never seen him before. He had a California license plate. He wanted gas and Myra came out. The man got out of the car and talked while she operated the pump.

"Big truck in the ditch below here," he said.

"That so?" said Myra.

"Yep!" said the man. "One of them big logging trucks that hog the roads up here in Oregon. Comin' round a switchback, that guy dumped his load out over the bank. Serves him right, I say!"

"Too bad," said Myra. "Accidents do happen."

Joel heard it all.

"What color was the logging truck, mister?" he asked.

The man hesitated.

"Blue?" asked Joel. "That's Empire Logging Company. Yellow? That's Johnson's. Green? That's Skinner's. Orange? That's my Uncle Irv's. It wasn't orange, was it?"

"Don't remember," said the man.

"It couldn't be orange," said Joel, " 'cause my Uncle Irv's a good driver. He's never had an accident."

The man frowned.

"There's always a first time, you know," he said.

Then he grinned, as if it was funny.

Myra went in the store to get the man's change. Joel remembered Jinx and how she had run away.

"You didn't happen to see a little girl goin' down the road, did you, mister?" he asked. "Short hair, long legs and . . ."

"Why yes," said the man. "I did see this kid a-streakin' down the road as if somethin' was chasin' her. Had a suitcase in her hand. Seemed kinda funny to me, but . . ."

Myra came out again, and Joel turned away.

He didn't want Myra to hear. The man got in his Chevvy and drove off.

Joel knew all he needed to know. Jinx had gone south. So now he'd have to follow her. She had a good head start. Could he catch up with her? He hoped she had sense enough not to be a hitch-hiker and hitch a ride with somebody. Then he'd never find her.

He started off down the road, walking as fast as he could go. He had not gone far when he heard a loud motor roaring behind him. It was a low-boy carrying a cat. The driver was Wallie Whitcomb from River Bend gas station. He must be going to the wrecked logging truck.

Joel signaled. Wallie pulled up and the boy jumped on. This would be faster. Now maybe he could catch up with Jinx.

He rode with Wallie to the scene of the accident. The first thing he saw before he jumped off was the color of the logging truck. It was not orange, so it was not Uncle Irv. Joel was thankful for that. It was yellow. That was the Johnson Logging Company.

Before they got off, Wallie leaned over and said to Joel: "One of them cowboy drivers! College kid, still green behind the ears! Likes to go fast round the corners. Can't tell them bright kids a thing. They know it all."

The driver was a young fellow, who looked pretty scared.

"I was only goin' sixty," he said.

"Limit for loggin' trucks is fifty," growled Wallie. "And you better make it twenty round these hairpin turns."

"Well, I got to get there," said the driver. "I'm fightin' for time all the time, got to make three trips a day. It's fifty-six miles from the landing to the mill, that's a hundred and twelve miles round trip, besides the stops for loading and unloading, besides the traffic, cars crawlin' in and out and tryin' to pass, and construction and red lights. It makes a very long day, unless I speed up a little."

"Speedin' up can land you in the ditch," said Wallie, "or even land you in jail."

Wallie set to work with his cat to pick the logs up. Then he would hoist the truck back to the road again and load the logs back on.

Joel watched, fascinated.

He sat with the driver on a stone by the road. The driver was friendly and talked. He said it was his first summer out of college and he aimed to make big money driving the logging truck. He wanted to go back to college again in the fall.

"But I thought you graduated," said Joel.

"I did," said the young man. "But now I want to do some postgraduate work in engineering. Just college is not enough."

"It's not?" asked Joel.

They had a nice talk and Joel liked the fellow even if he had tried to speed going around a corner.

"Golly! I forgot!" said Joel suddenly. "I gotta go hunt for my sister. She ran away from home."

The young man stared. "She what?"

"Ran away from home," said Joel. "Jinx is always doing crazy things. I'm hunting for her, I'm gonna bring her back. Want to get her there before Dad gets home from work or she'll be in trouble. You didn't see her, did you?"

"Seems like I passed some kids along the road," said the young man, "but I'm not sure. Where's she goin'?"

"How do I know?" asked Joel. "A man in a Chevvy told me he saw her headin' for Medford, or she might go to Rogue River where my aunt lives."

He got up and started off.

"Hope you find her," said the young man.

Joel hated to leave the wrecked log-load, but marched sturdily on. He rounded a curve and followed the highway as it started up a steep winding hill. He stopped and got a drink at a spring bubbling out from the side of the hill. He saw footprints —a girl's sneakers.

She's been here! Joel said to himself. *Those are her tracks. She stopped for a drink of water.* If she walked all the way from home, without getting a lift, she musta been tired and thirsty by the time she got here. So maybe she didn't go much farther.

Maybe she stopped to camp in the woods.

No, Jinx was scared of the woods. She would never sleep out

all night, alone. She'd go to somebody's house and ask for food and a bed, I bet. She'd rather sleep in some stranger's house than out in the woods with the wild animals.

Then Joel happened to think: But there are no houses along here. Not a single house all the way over the mountain. Nothing but woods.

Joel kept to the road. She must be on the road ahead somewhere. He trudged steadily on. The road was uphill and he went slowly taking deep breaths. Several cars passed, but none stopped.

Part way up the mountain was a Recreation Park maintained by the Forest Service. She might be there. It had some tables and benches for picnicking, outdoor fireplaces, and several shelters. Even there it would be too spooky for Jinx to sleep out, but at least she might be resting, and if so, he could catch up with her.

Golly! He just had to get her home and get her home quick, before Mom and Dad got back. They'd be upset to find her run away.

But where was that girl?

There were no clues of any kind. Only guesswork. She *might* have come this way. But if a car picked her up, he'd never get her.

Joel saw a Forest Service truck parked in a lane by the road. It was filled with paint cans. He went in and talked to the man. The man said this unit had been sold for salvage logging. He was marking the trees to be cut with a slash of blue paint.

Joel asked, "Did you see a girl go by, walking? Small, short hair?"

"No," said the man. "I been in the woods painting."

The boy went back to the road again and started on. Up ahead he saw something funny. It looked like a flag flying above a tree. A white flag tied on a stick. What on earth? Was this some new kind of signal used by the Forest Service—for spraying or dusting? Something new that Joel did not know about?

He went up closer.

It was a madrone tree—a beauty, with several graceful curving red trunks. The dark green leaves were shiny and beautiful and made a thick canopy at the top. Above them, the white flag was sticking out.

Joel stared, and as he stared, the flag began to wave up and down. Was somebody up there signaling? If so, to whom? Joel had never seen anything like this before.

Then he heard a sound. *Yoo-hoo! Yoo-hoo!*

"Golly!" cried Joel. "Somebody's up there!"

At the same minute he saw on the ground a battered suitcase, lying open. He went up closer. He went under the tree and looked up. Over the branches hung an array of girl's clothes—dresses, slips, nightgowns, and underthings.

"JINX! You come right down here!" cried Joel angrily. "Are you crazy or what?"

"No," said Jinx. "I'm glad to see you. Come on in my house. I'm living in a tree now. This is my home."

"What's your flag for?" asked Joel, curious.

"Distress signal," said Jinx.

"Are you in distress?" asked Joel.

"No," said Jinx, "just playing a game. I didn't want you to go past."

"You're cuckoo!" said Joel. "How did you know I was coming?"

"I knew you'd come to find me."

"What if I hadn't?" asked Joel.

"I'd a slept in this tree all night," said Jinx. "My bedroom's up here. I had a nice nap this afternoon."

"You can't sleep in a tree, you'd fall out," said Joel.

"But I didn't," said Jinx. "I laid my coat on two limbs and went to sleep. To hold on, I braced my feet. My hands would drop off, but my feet were braced, so I didn't fall."

"O.K., come on home now," said Joel. "Here I had to come all this long way to find you, and I had no idea where you went. Please be sensible and come on home."

But Jinx insisted on staying where she was.

"I'm not going home," she said. "I live here now."

"Now Jinx, you know you're just showing off," said Joel. "You pulled this stunt just to get out of potato-bug picking. It's not gonna help one bit. Tomorrow there'll be twice as many potato bugs on your vines as today. You'll have to pick twice as long."

"I hate potato bugs," said Jinx.

"That's just too bad," said Joel, "but you have to pick them anyway. Running off won't help you to get out of it. When Dad says a thing, he means it."

Joel argued and argued with her, but the more he coaxed, the more determined Jinx was to stay. So at last in disgust he went off without her. He hurried back down the road till he came to the wrecked logging truck. The logs were being loaded back on the truck now.

"Did you find your sister?" asked the driver.

"Yes," said Joel.

"Where?"

"Living in a tree up on the mountain," said Joel, grinning. "She says it's her home. She's got all her clothes hanging on the branches. She's crazy."

"You gonna take her home?"

"She won't come," said Joel. "She's stubborn. So I'm goin'

home without her. At least I know where she is."

Wallie's work done, he turned the low-boy and started to go.

"Want a ride, Joel?" he asked.

"Sure!" said Joel, climbing on.

Like a rush of mighty wind, a girl came flying down the road and jumped in the cab beside him, suitcase and all.

"Don't go without me!" cried Jinx.

Wallie and Joel laughed. The young driver of the logging truck laughed, too.

But Jinx didn't.

"You spoiled my game," she said, sullenly.

Joel did not answer.

Jinx was sober now, thinking how silly had been her escapade. She did not say a word all the way back to the Drum Store, nor up the woods road. When she saw Dad's pick-up in the yard, and Mom at the kitchen door, she was scared. She turned to Joel and said, trembling: "I left a note on the kitchen table. Do you suppose . . ."

Joel pulled the crumpled note from his pants pocket.

"You don't need to tell them if you don't want to," he said. "I won't tell either."

But it was hard for Jinx to keep secrets.

She marched in and said, "Mom, I ran away from home today and Joel came and brought me back."

Dad heard it, too.

"I'm glad Joel's got some sense if you haven't," he said.

He bent over and kissed her.

The next day Jinx picked potato bugs.

Chapter Seven

THE RIDE

ONE night Uncle Irv stopped in and asked Joel if he'd like to have a ride on his logging truck.

"Sure!" said Joel. "When?"

"Tomorrow," said Uncle Irv. "I'll take one load to the mill first and pick you up on my way back to the woods, at nine-thirty. You be down at the store ready. Be sure to bring your lunch. You'll be plenty hungry before you get back."

Joel was always ready for a ride on the big truck. He enjoyed it now even more than when he was younger. Each time the trip was as great an adventure as it had been when he was six.

Mom packed a lunch for him and he ran down the woods road as fast as he could go. He waited at the roadside, but not for long.

Through the morning stillness, Joel could hear the sound of a truck motor getting louder and louder. The next moment the big diesel was there, grinding to a halt. In the cab sat Uncle Irv, grinning. He wore a blue T-shirt and a visor cap, tilted back. Quickly he pulled Joel up in the high seat beside him, with no time lost. There the boy sat like a king, looking down on the immense hood and watching the road ahead being sucked under the mighty truck.

Joel looked at Uncle Irv and smiled. There was so much noise and vibration, they could not talk. Uncle Irv kept shifting the gears between the two seats.

Joel looked behind. The truck was a monster with sixteen wheels and could carry a load up to a hundred tons. It was empty now, without logs. The trailer with the rear wheels was riding on top of the body. They were heading for the woods to get the second load. The truck banged down the canyon road, took all the curves without slowing up and kept on going. Uncle Irv's strong arms were on the steering wheel every minute and had it under perfect control. Uncle Irv put a box of red cherries on the seat and he and Joel began to eat.

Before they knew it, they had left the highway and were on the gravel mountain road and climbing. Once they passed huge boulders in the road that had fallen from the high cliff at one side, and made the truck turn out. They came to one switchback after another, as the road ran in and out and around the mountains. It followed a devious track around one mountain and then another, climbing always higher and higher. Up the steep

grades the big truck slowed down to twenty miles per hour and seemed to barely crawl.

They were in National Forest now. That was where most of the logging was being done. The Forest Service auctioned off to the highest bidder the units of trees they wanted cut. The mills who bought the "sales" then hired gyppo logging companies to do the work. The good timber was harder and harder to get, so the units were on higher and higher ground. The Forest Service designated each unit for either "clear-cut" or "selective cutting." For a "clear-cut," everything had to be cut off, no trees of any kind left, and the snags and brush had to be burned afterwards. In some clear-cuts no burning was to be done.

The Forest Service justified burning for two reasons—to reduce the fire hazard caused by the slash or limbs, and to prepare the ground for tree seeding or planting. Burning was not done if there were established seedlings.

The Johnson Logging Company was making a clear-cut on a steep, precipitous slope on one of the highest points, 4500 feet. Uncle Irv was headed for this location. Big Joe was their hook-tender. He had climbed and rigged their spar-pole and now he was engineering the job.

Uncle Irv's truck ground its way steadily on. The road was a mere rocky ledge now on the edge of a deep precipice. A tiny stream could be seen down in the valley far, far below. On the other side, great trees lined the hillside and seemed to touch the sky. Across the valley Joel could see mountainsides still thick with timber, and others logged off, with stumps, logs, and slash left lying open to the sun.

"Why do they log so high up?" shouted Joel.

"Got to go where the timber is!" answered Uncle Irv. "As the crow flies, we're only about five miles from River Road. But by this woods road, it's fifteen or more."

The road was now so narrow there was no room for passing except at certain wider shoulders. The empty truck always took the outside, the loaded truck the inside. At one bad place, a loaded truck met them, coming away from the landing. Uncle Irv had to back to the shoulder to let it pass. A dog rode on the water-tank platform back of the cab. The driver, Jerry Watson, honked, the dog barked, and Uncle Irv waved. Joel sat there on his high perch, eating cherries like a king, spitting the pits out on the floor. He was happier than he'd been for a long time.

Uncle Irv pointed across the valley to a clear-cut.

"That's where we're going," he said.

But there were many more curves and rough places before they got there. And when they did, they came in from a higher level. At a switchback, Uncle Irv drove in forward, then backed down a long distance to the landing, so the truck would be facing out for leaving.

Now at last they were there, high, high up on the steep mountainside. Joel had never been so high before. Only high-lead logging could be done on a steep pitch like this. Cat-logging would not work here. The cats would roll. They could be used only on level ground.

Joel jumped down from the truck to stretch his legs. He

walked to the brink and sat down. Uncle Irv came too and pointed out the mountain peaks, some covered with snow, and told him their names. Joel looked for the logging crew but could not see them. Uncle Irv sent him back up the slope behind the landing to sit on a stump and watch.

"It's not safe to stay too close," he said. "Sometimes things go whizzing by when you don't expect them."

Dad and the crew were working on the steep slope below, out of sight. The pitch was so steep, they often had to hold onto trees or brush to keep their balance.

Joel sat down and looked around.

On the landing sat the donkey-engine and the shovel, one on each side of the spar-pole, which was heavily rigged with guy wires, spreading out in all directions, anchored to tree stumps. The machines were busy. The donkey-engine roared and clattered, whistles shrieked, men gave signals, and high overhead a cable went swinging carrying a dangling choker. It disappeared over the hillside, where the choker-setter waited till it settled, then fastened it round a log.

He scrambled out of the way, the whistle-punk gave a signal, the whistle sounded, and the log was lifted up into the air, snapping off small trees in its way. Up to the landing came the big log and found its place on a pile of others. The chaser unhooked the choker and stepped out of danger. The shovel-operator circled his boom around, picked up the log with his grappling hooks, circled back again, and set the log neatly on the waiting truck.

How exciting it was! What fun to watch!

Joel saw one large log after another come up as if by magic over the side of the mountain, all for Uncle Irv's truck. He loved the tangy odor of the freshly cut logs. Once during a delay, the chaser came up to talk to Joel.

"Why don't you come take a ride on one of them logs?" he asked.

"It might be a little bumpy," said Joel.

"You gonna be a logger like your dad?" he asked.

"Sure am," said Joel, grinning. "Couldn't be nothing else."

There were so many signals, so many piercing blasts of the air whistle, Joel could not keep track of them all. *One* meant *stop, no questions asked. Two* meant *go ahead—tight line. Three* meant *go back—slack line.* To the loggers, each blast spoke in a language they understood. It was as if the whistle talked to them, saying: "I'm coming!" "Watch out there!" "Be careful!" or sometimes even "Danger—watch *out!*" *Five* shrill blasts meant *"Accident,"* Joel knew, and he hoped he might never hear it.

Above the noisy din of the engines, the whistles, the roars and clatters, the whining of the blocks and cables, Joel could hear his father's booming voice—barking out orders, telling the men what to do. Everything depended on Dad, the hook-tender —the lives of all the men in the crew, the number of logs taken out in a day and the success of the whole logging enterprise. How proud he was of Dad!

Noon came, the whistle blew, the engines fell silent and the men stopped work. The crew came up over the brow of the hill—Dad, two choker-setters and the whistle-punk. The donkey-puncher, the chaser, and the shovel-operator all came, too. They brought their lunch buckets and Uncle Irv and Joel joined them.

There was Dad grinning, sweat and grime trickling down his face. His shirt was wet and dripping and his pants were covered with dust and pitch and grease and grime. Like those of the other men, his pants were stagged—cut off and fringed above his calk boots. His arms were strong with bulging muscles. What a wonderful thing to be a logger like Dad.

The men crowded in a shady spot beside the logging truck to eat lunch. They opened their tightly packed lunch buckets and began to gobble. Meat sandwiches, hard-boiled eggs, apples, and hunks of cheese quickly disappeared. Then the jokes began.

When Joel opened his bucket, out jumped a bullfrog!

"Now who . . . ?" There was no use asking. Joel turned red in the face and the men laughed.

They passed a can of Copenhagen around and helped theirselves. They began to brag about who could jump farther, run faster, eat more, fight harder, yell louder than anyone else.

"Golly!" said Eddie Wykoff, the new choker-setter. "One of my leg's gettin' shorter than the other!"

"That's from workin' on the steep slope," said Jake, the shovel-operator. "Never thought you'd be loggin' vertical, didja?"

"Naw," said Eddie. "I like to be on the level."

"More fun when it's straight up and down," said Big Joe.

"Put a cat on that pitch," said George Barker, the other choker-setter, "it'd turn a somersault and land in the creek at the bottom of the canyon."

"Almost did that myself," said Eddie. "Lost my balance once, felt myself a-goin', grabbed a little tree and held on tight!"

The men laughed.

"How come the Forest Service wants a clear-cut here?" asked Jake. "They can't replant. Seed would be washed out and there's no soil for roots of young trees."

"Douglas fir won't grow in the shade," said Eddie. "That's why they make a clear-cut."

"But Douglas fir trees got to have plenty of water or they'll die," said Big Joe. "How can you keep 'em wet on a slope in the boiling sun?"

"Waste o' time all that re-seeding and planting by hand," said Lou Weston, the donkey-puncher. "Selective cutting is better . . ."

"Provided you don't kill all the little trees gettin' the big ones out," said George.

"Best way is to leave some old trees to re-seed theirselves," insisted Lou. "Be faster, too, and not take so much of the tax-payer's money."

"They're crazy to burn it off after a clear-cut," said Jake. "Soil can't stand those high temperatures, nothin' will ever grow there again."

Al Duncan, the chaser, spoke up.

"You'll never see a planted forest come to maturity, mark my words!" he said. "It just makes fodder for the next forest fire. All that fresh green stuff burns like tissue paper."

Eddie Wykoff looked thoughtful, but said nothing.

"What bothers me," said Big Joe, "the government won't let

nature have its way. Those Forest Service boys are great for
poison, they've gone crazy on spraying. Anything that eats tree
seed, they say is an enemy. So they spray and kill the birds,
chipmunks, rabbits, and wild life. It's plumb crazy."

"Thinnin' out the timber in selective logging is no good either," Al Duncan went on. "Look at the old forests. Best timber
grows thick, close together, no side branches. There you get the
longest, straightest, finest logs, no knots. That's the timber
brings the best price."

"Well, boys," said Big Joe, "too bad the Forest Service don't
ask a good bunch o' loggers like us for advice. Just remember
them little ole college boys down there knows a lot more than
we do, 'cause they read it in a book! Let's get back to work."

Eddie got up and his left foot gave way under him. He began
to limp.

"Told you one leg's got shorter than the other . . ."

George Barker, the other choker-setter, had dropped off to
sleep.

"We got a dead man here," said Lou Weston. "Bring me a
rose, Joel, to put on his ear."

Whatever they said was funny. Joel roared with laughter and
George woke up.

"No more foolin'," said Big Joe. "Them logs down over the
brink are waitin' for us."

He turned to Joel.

"Son," he said, "you better help Uncle Irv chain up them logs
so they don't fall off his truck!"

"O.K.," said Joel, grinning. "I sure will."

"You goin' all the way to White City to the Mill with him?" asked Dad.

"Oh, sure!" said Joel. "I wouldn't miss that for anything."

"O.K.," said Dad.

Dad was glad to have Joel here. He wanted to boy to learn all he could about logging.

The load was not ready yet. Another log was needed to top it off. So Joel waited.

The men went back to their places. The engines began to rattle and bang, the whistles shrieked, the cable flew overhead with the choker on the end. More noise, more signals, but the log did not come up.

What was wrong? Joel waited impatiently. He was eager to

go. Uncle Irv stood by, restless too, watching.

Then came five sharp whistle blasts. Five shrill blasts—one, two, three, four, five, one after the other. The machines on the landing shut down at once. The chaser ran over and talked to the shovel-operator.

Something was wrong.

Joel looked at Uncle Irv, his heart beating fast.

"Somebody hurt?" He could hardly say the words.

Uncle Irv stood stiff and tense.

"Just some trouble down over the hill," he said. "Maybe a snag fell or the log got caught on something . . . lots of things can happen. Might be a widow-maker or . . ."

Uncle Irv was putting him off, Joel could tell. He was trying to keep him from knowing the truth.

Something had happened. Somebody was hurt. The silence was ominous. Overhead a big bird flew. Was it an eagle? A buzzard? Joel knew all about accidents. People pretended they were not afraid, but they were, deep down underneath. Why, any minute somebody could trip and fall down that steep pitch into the canyon. Eddie had joked about it, but . . .

Somebody was hurt, Joel knew it. *But not Dad. It couldn't be Dad. O God, don't let it be Dad. Dad's too strong, too brave, too careful. Dad's not afraid of anything. Dad's been hurt before, all those concussions and broken ribs and . . . It can't be Dad. But if it isn't, it must be somebody else.* Was Joel wishing that somebody else was hurt just so Dad would be safe? *Maybe a snag just bopped somebody on the head. That's nothing, it could happen to anybody. Maybe they just needed a new saw down there under the hill. Somebody broke the old one.*

Yes, that was it. They needed a saw.

The whistles shrieked again. Six times! Six sharp blasts. Joel counted—one, two, three, four, five, six.

He looked. Lou Weston, the donkey-puncher, was taking the saw down to them. *That was it. They needed a saw.*

But no, it wasn't a saw. It was a stretcher. Jake was helping. Down over the brink they went.

The air was still now. No machines rattling and banging. Only the song of a bird, a lilting happy song to rend a boy's heart. *Somebody hurt. Not Dad—don't let it be Dad, not Dad.* Joel kept saying it over and over. He stood there like a statue.

Uncle Irv had gone. He had left him and gone over to talk to Jake. They waited at the edge. It seemed an age. Then as last the stretcher came up, vertically. It had a man tied on it.

Joel could not look. He ran to the logging truck and climbed up into the cab. He sat there, dry-eyed and fearful, his heart pounding. He did not know it, but he was now, at twelve, experiencing the hardest part of a logger's life, the reality of danger.

Uncle Irv found him there. Uncle Irv was smiling, so it wasn't Dad, after all.

"That crazy kid, Eddie, almost rolled down the canyon," said Uncle Irv. "He had a bum ankle and then he let that log roll on it . . ."

At last Joel could speak. Relief came in a flash.

"Did it get mashed?" he asked.

"Not too bad," said Uncle Irv. "They'll take him to the hospi-

tal and put a cast on it. They're puttin' him in the crummy now."

It wasn't Dad, after all. How thankful Joel was!

"You still want to go to the mill with me?" asked Uncle Irv.

"Sure," said Joel.

The load of trouble left as fast as it came.

Joel climbed down from his seat to help Uncle Irv. The last log did not get loaded, so Uncle Irv decided to go without it. Joel carried the heavy chains to him and watched as he threw them over the logs and tightened the binders with the swede.

Then they were ready to start.

They climbed in the truck again. Taking off up the shill, Joel reached out to some bushes and grabbed a branch.

"Better throw that out," said Uncle Irv. "That's poison oak. Remember: 'Leaves in three, let them be!' "

Going up the steep grade, the loaded truck seemed to barely crawl. Then it reached the highest point on the peak of the mountain and began the long, slow, and devious trip downward to the valley. In and out and around the mountains, most of the time on a rocky shelf ledge, the huge truck made its careful way.

Down on the valley road, Uncle Irv had to make two stops. The first was at the scaling station, where the logs were measured and the number of board feet estimated. The other was at the weighing station, where the load was weighed.

When they passed the Drum Cash Store, no one Joel knew was in sight, but Uncle Irv sounded his horn anyway. Then there was still another mountain to crawl over and in and around, before they got to White City. Joel dozed most of the way, so when the truck stopped, he woke with a start. Uncle Irv took the chains off and the logs were quickly dumped into the millpond, making a great splash. Joel watched from his seat in the cab.

On the way home, Uncle Irv told him about one bad curve in the road called Devil's Elbow, and how many trucks loaded with logs had gone over the bank. Joel told Uncle Irv about the truck driven by the college boy.

Once Uncle Irv's truck skidded off to one side, but Uncle Irv quickly pulled it back on the road again.

"What's the matter?" asked Joel. "You gettin' sleepy?"

"No," said Uncle Irv. "Didn't you see that deer?"

"A deer?" asked Joel. "Where?"

"Gone in the woods now," said Uncle Irv. "If I'd a hit him, we'd a had a nice mess o' venison for the freezer."

Joel laughed.

Uncle Irv stopped in front of the Drum Store to let Joel off. He ran home all the way up the woods road.

Chapter Eight

THE FIRE

"Ow, ow, ow!" Joel hopped around on one foot, dripping with water. Jinx stood by, holding an empty bucket in her hand.

"I burned myself! *Ow, ow, ow!* Don't touch me!" screamed Joel.

Mom came up to see. Joel had to stand still and explain.

"Well, I had matches in my pocket . . ."

"Now you know, Joel, you're not to take matches," Mom began.

"My knife musta rubbed against a match in my pocket and lighted it and set me on fire and burned my leg!"

"And your pants, too," said Mom. "I can smell the cloth."

"I put it out, I doused water on him," cried Jinx.

"She threw a whole bucket of water on my head," said Joel,

laughing. "My head wasn't on fire, my pants were. She almost drownded me!"

Mom put salve on the burned spot and made Joel change his pants.

"Now don't you go to carryin' matches again, hear?" she said. "You want to burn yourself up? Or do you want to start a forest fire?"

Joel shook his head, sober now. Forest fires were no joke, not to a logger, nor to his son. Forest fires could wipe a man out and leave him with nothing. Joel knew that.

This was his third bad burn. He had had two before. Last winter he got a burn on his backside, from backing up too close against the heater. It was a cold day for Oregon. There was a whole foot and a half of snow, the most Joel had ever seen in his whole life and he thought his feet were going to freeze off. That's why he got that burn—just trying to get warm.

Then on another cold day, he got a burn on his stomach from spilling hot coffee. It would not have happened if Jinx had not tried to grab the cup of hot coffee out of his hand. He was trying to get warmed up inside, that time, just drinking something hot.

But this time—how those matches ever got struck and set fire to his pants was a mystery. He could only blame it on his knife, his trusty knife. His knife was useful for a hundred jobs, so he always had it with him.

"Joel, run down to the store and get the mail," said Mom. "And here's a list. Pick up these groceries."

Joel wandered down the woods road, taking his own time. His bike was broken now, beyond repair. He stopped once to throw

a stone at a bluejay, but did not hit it. He peeked under the culvert to see if Jinx's rainbow trout were still there. But they were gone. Somebody must have fished them out and eaten them.

He strolled across the highway and came to the store. Just then a big logging truck came round the curve, a blue one. That was the Empire Logging Company. He was ready to signal to the driver, when the truck braked to a stop. The driver stuck his head out and called:

"Fire at Tiller! Woods on fire!"

The man did not wait, just drove on again. Had Joel heard right? Did the man say *woods on fire?*

Joel did not wait either. He banged into the store.

There sat Myra Ross at the counter reading a book. She was always reading a book, or writing something in a tablet. Sometimes she pounded a typewriter in the back room. She wrote up the local news for the Myrtle Creek weekly paper.

"The woods is on fire!" cried Joel. "Over by Tiller!"

Myra did not look up. She kept on reading.

"I tell you the woods is on fire!" shouted Joel.

Myra looked up, unperturbed.

"I heard you the first time," she said quietly.

"It's a forest fire—over by Tiller," Joel went on.

"Did somebody set it?" asked Myra.

"I don't know," said Joel.

"Or drop a cigarette?"

"I don't know," said Joel.

"Or did a boy have matches in his pocket?"

"I don't know. The man didn't say," said Joel.

"Who told you?"

"That truck driver, on that blue truck," said Joel. "That's the Empire Logging Company."

Myra didn't seem to care. Forest fires meant nothing to her. She wasn't a logger. She often bragged about how she had never been in the woods to see the men falling or bucking or getting the logs out. All she did was read and write. Joel rushed out the door and banged it hard behind him. He'd like to knock the store over, he'd show her!

There was no one around. No cars parked by the store as usual. No one coming in to buy groceries or coming out with their arms full of paper bags. Where the heck was everybody, anyhow?

Joel rushed up the woods road to tell Mom. On the way, he began to feel guilty. Had he and Billy put their campfire out

properly? Did they take the time to douse it the second time?
He could not remember. It was a long time ago, but maybe the
fire had been smoldering all this time, and finally broke out just
above Tiller. All at once his pants pocket felt hot. The matches
in his pocket were burning him again. Or was it only imagina-
tion? That's right—Mom had taken them away from him.

"Where are the groceries?" asked Mom.

"The woods is on fire, Mom! Over back of Tiller!" shouted
Joel.

"Oh, no!" cried Mom. "It can't be."

She would not believe it until Joel explained how he knew.
Sandy and Jinx listened, eyes and mouths wide open.

Mom refused to take the news seriously.

"Good thing it rained last night," she said. "It was only a
sprinkle, but every drop helps. Bad thunder and a lot of lightning. Maybe it will rain again."

"The sky's looking dark," said Sandy. "The sun's gone under."

"Oh, I'm sure it's gonna rain *hard!*" cried Jinx.

They were just talking to ease their fears.

"Dad's been worried the last couple of days," Mom went on.
"He said if the humidity went any lower, the men would be
ordered out of the woods again. Too much risk. The woods is as
dry as tinder. It's typical forest fire weather."

Joel went outside. The sky did seem to be getting a little
darker now. More rain would put the fire out, but not a drop
came. Only lightning. Lightning flashed again and again. All the
loggers dreaded lightning. It could start a dozen fires. It always
struck the dead snags.

Joel ran back to the kitchen door.

"Mom, I'm going to hitch a ride on a logging truck and go and tell Dad." Joel wanted to see Dad as soon as possible.

"No, you're not," said Mom. "No use goin' there. Dad'll find it out soon enough. Go back down to the store and get those groceries. Tell Myra that if the women are needed to let me know. Tell her to send word to Dot Kramer and Lizzie Borden. And ask if she's got plenty of coffee in stock."

There were no telephones, so messages had to be sent by word of mouth.

Joel was glad to go to the store again. It was the best place to hear all the latest news.

He ran in at the door. Myra was talking to two strange men and Joel listened. The fire had started at Day's Creek and was now on the hills back of Tiller. Lightning had struck in two or three places—that was what caused it. The fire was headed south. The Forest Service had all their men out.

The strangers left and Joel asked, "Myra, you got plenty coffee?"

Myra nodded, so he went out again. Then he remembered the rest of the message. He went back in.

"Mom says send word to Dot Kramer and Liz Borden," the boy said. "Mom says she'll come if you need her."

"O. K.," said Myra.

He pulled the list out of his pocket.

"Mom wants these groceries," he said.

Myra took the list and began putting things in paper sacks. Joel waited, standing first on one foot, then another. He wondered why she was so slow. How could she be so slow, when there was a fire going on?

"Why are you so pokey?" he asked. "Don't you know the woods is burning up?"

Myra did not answer.

"Charge it," said Joel. He picked up the grocery bags and rushed home.

There was no word from Dad. Mom said he had probably been called off his job and was helping to fight the fire.

At home with Mom and the girls, Joel could learn nothing. So again he went to the store. The store was the center of information. People came there to bring and to hear the latest news. If there was any news, the store was the place to hear it.

Snuff Carter and Jim Hunter came up, but they knew nothing. Then Billy Weber appeared and Billy had news. He said more fires were starting. It had kept on drizzling and lightning flashed off and on. The lightning was starting one fire after another. The fire had come up the canyon to Tiller, run along the ridge behind the church, jumped the South Umpqua River, and was now back up behind the Forest Service Station.

"Oh, gosh!" said Joel. "Then it's coming up this way—up towards Dad's timber. Is your dad out fire-fighting, Billy?"

"Naw," said Billy. "He says it's no use."

"No use?" cried Joel. "No use savin' the woods? Savin' the trees for your dad and mine to log and get paid for?"

"Dad says once a fire starts, it's got to run its course," said Billy.

A Forest Service man drove up, stopped and went into the store. The boys recognized Bob Downey. A crowd of people had gathered.

Bob said the fire was moving fast. He said it was hard to fight because the units were far apart. They needed men with cats and bulldozers to push fire trails in a dozen places. Joel started to speak to him, but Bob was too busy to listen. He drove off.

"I bet my dad will go and help," said Joel. "He's probably there already. My dad's not afraid of anything—not even of a forest fire."

Billy said nothing.

Jinx and Sandy came down the road. They had cookies and potato chips with them, and gave some to the boys.

About noon, cars drove up and several women got out, children too. Joel saw Mom, Dot Kramer, Lizzie Borden, and others he knew. They had had Myra's message and brought food supplies with them. Myra's kitchen, which opened off at one side of the store, was soon a busy place. The women made coffee and prepared sandwiches. They talked about the fire and gossiped about their neighbors. Children ran in and out, laughing and crying.

"I'm hungry," said Joel. "I'm goin' in to see what I can find."

"Get me something to eat, too," said Billy.

When he came out Joel had a bulging paper sack, and his hands full of candy bars and popsicles.

"Whew!" said Billy. "You made a big haul."

"You bet I did!" said Joel. "Mom told me to help myself."

The two boys went down to the creek back of the store to eat. They took their shoes off and sat on rocks with their feet in the water. They ate greedily. Everything tasted good. The popsicles had to be eaten first before they melted.

"Bet you had to pay for these," said Billy.

"No," said Joel, "I don't have any money. I just charged them, like groceries. Myra didn't like it much, but a person can't go hungry when a forest fire's going on."

After they ate, Joel got up and looked around. He found some small white bones lying in the grass.

"Look at this, Billy," he said.

Billy came to look. It was the skeleton of an animal.

"Here's its legs all together," said Joel. "There's the body."

"There's the head and the neck and the jaws and teeth," said Billy.

"What do you think it is?" asked Joel.

"A beaver, I bet," said Billy. "There's a tree he chawed down." Near by was the stump of a tree.

"Myra said there was a beaver down here," said Joel. "I re-

member how mad she got when it chawed down the post for her clothesline and all her clothes went down in the mud!"

The boys laughed.

"This will be fine for my museum," said Billy. "Gimme that paper sack." He put the bones inside. "I've got ten snake rattles, some old coins, some fish bones, birds' nests, and a lot of stuff already."

"There comes the Forest Service!" cried Joel. "Let's go see."

A Forest Service truck drew up, filled with supplies—hoes, axes, shovels, and piles of blankets. The driver went in the store and asked again for volunteers—loggers with cats and bull-dozers to scoop dirt and lay back-fires. He wanted men.

But there were no men at the store, only women. The women said their men were already in the woods. They gave him all the sandwiches and food they had ready.

When the Forest Service man came out of the store, the boys asked him, "Can we go with you? We want to see the fire. We'll help fight it."

"No," said the man. He jumped in his truck and rode off.

By this time the sky up above the ridge was red. Smoke filled the air, darkened the valley and blotted out the sun. Lightning flashed. No logging trucks came by. The highway seemed quiet and deserted without them. People stood around at the store, talking quietly and watching the sky. Jinx and Sandy and the Kramer girls were there, talking and laughing, as if there was no forest fire at all. The boys hung around and waited. They didn't quite know what they were waiting for. But they could not leave the store.

Late that afternoon, Matt Weber, Billy's father, drove up in a truck and got out. Another man, Ben Watson, drove up in a beat-up old car. Ben was a good faller. He used to fall with Big Joe. Ben's unshaven face was covered with soot and grime, his eyes were bloodshot, and his clothing was torn. Billy's dad went to the car window to talk.

"You look like you been through the war," said Matt.

"Worse'n that," said Ben. "I been through hell fire! How come you ain't fire-fightin'?"

"I hate that job as much as you do," said Matt. "Every logger hates fire-fightin'."

"But some of us got to do it," said Ben. "I'm sick and tired of it. We just git one fire under control and another one starts. Those old dead snags are hollow and got pitch at the bottom. They're just waitin' for a torch, they go up like a chimney.

Lightning keeps strikin' 'em. The Forest Service needs all the men they can get. You gonna come help us, Matt?''

"Nope," said Billy's dad. "It's all a waste o' time. When the woods is a furnace, men can't do a thing. Two hundred acres burning sky-high, no man can stop it. Only heavy rain. When it gets into the crowns of the trees, that crazy fire goes leaping from treetop to treetop, and then the burning branches fall and set fire to everything on the ground. It's no place for a man, I say. There's not a thing a man can do to stop a fire once it gets going. He wears himself out, but that don't stop the fire.''

"You won't fight to save the woods," said Ben Watson, "even if it means your livelihood and feedin' your own family?''

"I won't volunteer," said Matt, "and if they draft me, I'll go but I won't work. I'm not the only one and you know it. Most of the loggers feel as I do. That's why so many walk off the job.''

The men's words were sharp now. Was there going to be a fight? Ben Watson got mad easy. He was known as a ready fighter. But this time he only spoke, and his words were as sharp as a knife.

"Some men are just quitters!" he said, and drove off.

Billy's dad was mad, too. He called to Billy and they got in the truck and left.

"Oh, here's your sack!" cried Joel, running after the truck. "You forgot your bones, Billy.''

But Billy was gone, so Joel kept the sack. He would take good care of it until he saw Billy again.

When Mom left the store, she called to the girls and Joel. She made them all go home with her. She went home and started supper. Pretty soon Uncle Irv drove up in his pick-up. He was dirty and tired and worn. He looked as if he hadn't slept for ages.

"I can't stay but a minute," he said. "They're trailin' the fire now, to hold it. Big Joe told me to come and tell you. He won't be comin' home tonight. The Forest Service came and took him off his job. They need all the fallers they can get. Where he's workin', the trees are all on fire, and he's falling them, to keep the fire from spreading."

"Falling burning trees?" cried Mom.

"Yes," said Irv. "It's got to be done."

"Did they get the food?" Mom asked.

"Yes, there's plenty of food and everything," said Irv. "The Forest Service is right on the job. They're stayin' right there, where the worst fire is, in charge. Trouble is it's been jumpin' from one place to another, and that's bad. At least twenty-one fires have started from this lightning. The Forest Service planes are out checking all locations."

Then he added, "Big Joe says he can't leave tonight, 'cause so many men walked off the job."

"Walked off?" said Mom.

"They don't like fightin' other people's fires," said Irv. "They lose money leavin' their own jobs. They need every day's wage they can get in summer, before winter comes and logging stops and they can't earn a penny. You know how it is."

"But the Forest Service pays them, don't they?" asked Mom.

"Sure, but they like to gripe," said Irv. "Every logger just detests and loathes and hates fightin' fires and everybody knows it, though some won't admit it. So they quit when the Forest Service is not looking."

Mom said, "I can't understand it. It's hard work, but . . ."

"Some are like Big Joe," said Irv. "They don't leave. They eat and sleep and stay by a fire till it's plumb out." He paused a minute, then went on, "I almost forgot. It's different with Joe, you see. He's fightin' for himself, not for somebody else. Big Joe said to tell you the fire's movin' over to his timber. That's why he can't leave!"

It was bad news and Irv did not wait to see how his sister liked it. He jumped in his truck and rattled off.

Mom sank down in a chair and covered her face with her hands.

"It's in Dad's timber!" she said. Then she began to cry.

Jinx and Sandy put their arms around her. Joel stomped out of the house, he felt so bad about it.

But there was nothing they could do.

The next day was the longest one Joel ever lived through. The sky was overcast but the hoped-for rain did not come. In the air all through the valley was the heavy smell of burning wood and smoke. The smoke was so heavy it was hard to see and harder to breathe. The men did not come back, although others went to relieve them. Mom was sick with worry, but did not talk much.

At midday, Billy Weber came over and he and Joel decided to go up the mountain to see what was going on. Joel was worried about Dad's timber. Perhaps they could get close enough to see just how bad the fire was. They had not gone far when they heard a shout. Jinx came running up behind them.

"I'm going, too," she said.

The children did not talk much as they made the hard climb. At last they came to the range where the cows were. The cows were huddled in one corner, as if they sensed something wrong.

The children climbed the fences and went on toward the big woods. Soon they saw signs of trouble.

Cats and bulldozers had been through and cleared roadways on the edge of the mountain. This was National Forest now and the children could see ahead a large burned-over section. Fallen trees and brush tangles had been turned to ashes. The fire had moved on, leaving behind a scene of desolation. Ahead, in the tall woods, smoke was rolling high, flames flared up at intervals and the heavy smell of burning wood filled the air. Machinery and men were over beyond. The children stood still and looked.

"That's Dad's timber over there," said Joel, pointing. "It looks like the fire's there already."

"The wind's blowing it that-a-way," said Billy.

"But the rain will come and stop it," said Jinx, hopefully. "I'm sure it will. Look! Oh, look at the animals!"

Off to one side the children saw a stream of animals moving— rabbits, squirrels, chipmunks, mice, raccoons, and behind them a small herd of deer. They were singed and frightened, running away from the fire. They came out of the burning woods and ran down a steep bank, crossing over a woods road. They ran into the unburned part of the forest. A few stragglers followed behind.

"Oh, I hope they won't get burned up!" cried Jinx.

"The men are stopping the fire," said Joel. "And it sure looks

like rain. As soon as it rains, the men can come home and rest easy."

"Dark sky's not clouds," said Billy. "It's smoke."

"Oh, if only the rain would come . . ." wailed Jinx.

The children had no heart to go farther. They turned back and made their way slowly home. Billy took his shortcut and Jinx and Joel went into the house.

"When do we eat?" asked Joel.

"I smell something," said Jinx, "but it's not very appetizing. Something's dead around here."

Mom was busy at the stove, cooking.

"I've been smelling it all day long," Mom said. "It must be a dead mouse."

The children looked but no mouse could be found.

Joel turned to Jinx.

"How about the chipmunks?" he asked. "Did you let them die?"

Jinx looked in the shoebox under the davenport. All three were sleeping soundly.

"They're O. K.," she said.

Mom picked up a paper sack on the windowsill.

"Here are those sandwiches I gave you yesterday, Joel," she said. "Why didn't you eat them?"

She sniffed and looked inside the sack.

"Good grief!" cried Mom. "It's not sandwiches! It's stinkin' animal bones! The smell's enough to gag you!"

"Oh! Billy's beaver bones!" cried Joel. "Give 'em to me."

"Take them out and bury them," said Mom.

"But they're Billy's . . . for his collection, for his museum," said Joel.

"Bury them," said Mom, firmly.

And Joel did.

Not till the third night did the rain come, a short but heavy and welcome rain that put out all the fires and set men's, women's, and even children's fears at rest. It was very late when Dad came home. The family had all gone to bed, but they got up to hear his story.

The forest fire was over at last. It had taken a big bite out of Dad's timber, about twenty-five acres, but he was glad to have saved the rest.

Chapter Nine

THE BLOW

ONE Saturday, Joel met Eddie Wykoff down at the store. Eddie had a cast on his ankle, but was able to hobble around.

"You still got one leg shorter'n the other?" asked Joel.

"Sure, boy, sure!" said Eddie. "Time I get this blamed cast off, it'll be even shorter."

"You're not loggin' any more, Eddie, are you?" asked Joel.

"Well, not exactly what you call loggin'," said Eddie. "No more o' that choker-settin' for me. I don't like them choker-cables a-flyin' around like buzzards in the air and boppin' me on the head! No sir-ree, I got me a nice, soft, easy job."

"Doin' what?" asked Joel.

"Fire Watch!" said Eddie. "It's a cinch. Nothin' to do but read comics all day. I been doin' it every summer since I was fifteen.

Get paid, too—two dollars an hour, how's that? This year, when I got to be eighteen, I thought I'd get me a *man's* job and set chokers . . . but I didn't last long."

"You like spottin' fires better?" asked Joel.

"It's about all I can do and I was glad to get the job," said Eddie. "Ever since the Tiller fire, the Forest Service is more particular than ever. They're watchin' the mountains like a hawk, from now till the winter rains begin. They lost a lot of timber in the National Forest and they don't want it to happen again."

"Where's your Fire Watch?" asked Joel.

"Oh, up on top of Old Craggy, about five miles up that-a-way." Eddie waved his arm. "I used to ride my bike other summers, but now I can't with my clubfoot. I hitch a ride with Skinner's Logging truck. It's their outfit that's logging up there. Say, Joel, why don't you come along some day? I git lonesome up there—nobody to talk to. Come along, why don't you?"

"O.K.," said Joel. "I'd like to. When?"

"Monday afternoon, about three o'clock," said Eddie. "Be waitin' at the store and bring some lunch with you. Watch for the green logging truck. That's Skinner's. I'll be on it, lookin' for you. So long!"

The plan worked fine. Joel met the truck and hopped on. There was Eddie in the cab beside the driver. Joel had to hunch down in front. After a long and twisty ride up and down hill, they came to Eddie's location on the side of the mountain.

It was August now and the dry weather continued in this part of Oregon. The danger from forest fires increased. The loggers started "hoot-owling"—going to work at 2 or 3 A. M., to get in as many hours of work as possible before the sun came up and the humidity dropped. At their homes, they did their sleeping in the heat of the day, while the rest of the family was awake.

According to government regulations, every logging operation, no matter how small, had to have its own fire-fighting equipment. This meant a water-tank at the landing, fire tools for no other use in a sealed box, and spark arrestors on all exhaust pipes on machines. Besides this, a Fire Watch was employed to spot fires if any started.

Joel and Eddie jumped out of the truck. Joel looked around. The view from the landing was beautiful, steep canyons and more mountains beyond. He looked at Eddie's camp.

Eddie had things fixed up pretty nice. He had built a lean-to shelter and a table out of small logs. He had a box fitted out for keeping books and comics, and a small battery radio. Beside the table was a folding chair. Eddie had to sit on the landing and watch for fires. If he saw smoke anywhere, he had to call the Forest Service. There was a rig on the landing with a radio telephone in it.

"Would you like to be up in a lookout?" asked Joel.

"They don't man them all anymore," said Eddie. "The State Forests still have them, but the National Forests only a few. They find that airplanes are more useful for spotting fires."

"Do you just sit up here for three hours?" asked Joel.

"Oh, no," said Eddie. "After the crew leaves, I have to cover, on foot, on my bum foot, the area that was logged. I have to go over it all least twice. I have to go on foot to get the fire before it's out of control. I can put it out with a shovel and an axe and a

five-gallon can of water, if it's a little one."

The boys were both hungry, so they sat down to eat lunch. While they ate, Eddie talked about his work.

"Any machine can throw a spark," he said. "Friction on the lines can cause a fire. No matter what you do to prevent forest fires, it seems they start anyhow. The least little thing—a tiny spark—in dry weather like this, can sure cause trouble."

"Don't I know it!" said Joel. "That Tiller fire burned off hundreds of acres. Of course it was caused by lightning." He paused, then went on, "It must be fun stayin' up here in the woods every day."

"It gets lonesome," said Eddie. "I get tired readin' and listenin' to the radio, and wishin' something would happen. One day, what do you think I saw—a bear eating blackcaps! He just stood there and growled at me over the bushes, then turned and scooted off as fast as he could go. I've seen so many deer I can't count them all. Once I saw a doe with triplets! That was really something!"

Eddie turned the radio on and stretched out on the ground, his hands under his head.

"Well, if you're goin' to take a nap," said Joel, "I think I'll go watch the logging, before the men quit."

"O. K.," said Eddie, "but don't get lost. Them woods is big and it's mighty easy to get turned around."

"I'll be O. K.," said Joel.

"I have to make my rounds after a while," said Eddie. "I have to stay for three hours after the loggers leave. Then my brother comes for me in his Model A Ford. Be sure to get back here by that time."

Joel started out. How wonderful it was to be in the woods again. He had loved it all his life. He loved its peace and quiet, its flickering lights and half-shadows, the chirping and squeaking noises of the wildlife.

The tall trees of fir and pine and cedar made a curtain of green, reaching from the clouds down to the earth. Berries and ferns and wild flowers grew at their feet. Sometimes the fog drifted in over the mountaintops and draped itself over the low branches and dampened the pine and hemlock needles with drops of dew. The air was so clean and pure, scented with pines, good to fill the lungs. The earth was soft with a carpet of rotted and decaying trees and logs and leaves, with wild flowers springing up here and there.

Joel came out of the woods to the edge of a clear-cut and

stared. The contrast was frightening. The clear-cut was horrible, a scene of desolation. It was a vast area of amputated stumps, with chunks of waste wood strewn about, piles of slash and brush, and patches of hard naked soil showing. Small young trees had been broken off or damaged by the logging. Bare spots of rock or hard ground were not good places for seeds or seedlings to take hold. How could they ever replant in a place like this?

Joel came to the place where Skinner's men were working. He stopped to watch. They were falling a big Douglas fir tree. He heard the penetrating, angry buzz of the power saw long before he came up.

"DOWN THE HILL!" he heard the men shout.

First the shiver and the ominous cracking, and then the ter-

rifying roar as the mighty tree crashed down to earth and hit with a thundering thump. A shower of debris followed, twigs, branches, and vines.

Joel shivered. A rush of sorrow and regret swallowed him up. Why was it so tragic to see a tree fall? It hurt him horribly, although he knew it had to be. He had watched many trees fall, but this time it was different.

Out from the branches came dozens of silver flying squirrels. Joel had never seen so many in a flock before. When the tree started going, they all took off at once. With legs outspread like a big flat leaf, each squirrel began to glide through the air. It was a regular airlift! The whole flock made a dip down and then soared upward, ready to light on a nearby tree.

But there was no tree near. They went on and on, not too fast, gliding like birds with wings, like eagles . . .

Joel held his breath. How far could they go? A mile?

It must have been a mile across the clear-cut and over the deep valley, until they finally found a tree to their liking and settled in its branches. What cute little old things they were. And what a wonderful sight to see so many of them soaring!

How lucky they were!

When danger came, they could get out of the way. Mother Nature had provided them not with wings, but with a loose fold of fur-covered skin at each side of their bodies, which acted like sail when they spread their legs. Their furry tails were flat like feathers and helped them to balance and steer. What a wonderful arrangement it was.

They were night animals, Joel knew that. That was why they had such large bright eyes. They were cuter even than chipmunks. Jinx would like one for a pet, and she could probably tame it, too.

But making pets of wild things was foolish. You had to let them go back to the wild, or they would die. The three chipmunks were gone now. Joel was glad Jinx let them go before something happened to them. The woods was their best home, after all. Living with people was not good for them.

Joel thought of winter coming and the way the woods animals took care of themselves. They made nests or burrows or tunnels to live in. They stored food ahead of time, so they could eat, and some of them slept all winter, living off their own fat. The mice and the chipmunks and ground squirrels, and even the bears hibernated, but rabbits and deer had to live out in the snow. The cougar had his home in a cave in the rocks, Billy said. Billy knew a lot about animals. He had learned it from the animals themselves.

Joel came to a tree and saw bear manure at its base. Looking closely, he saw fresh claw marks on the bark. He looked around, but there was no sign of the bear.

He knew all the trees well, from the huge sugar pine with its cones a foot long, to the lacy hemlock, with its tiny inch-long cones. There was the stately Douglas fir, the ponderosa pine, the incense cedar, and the spruce. They were all beautiful. But his favorite was not one of the giants at all. It was the vine maple, a little delicate half-viney tree, with leaves of red and gold. There was always something red on it—leaves, twigs, and shoots, even its seed wings. And the madrone, too, with its smooth red bark, so easy to carve initials in, its thick shining leaves and edible red berries. Dad called it "the cleanest tree in the woods" because it was always shedding, "always changing its clothing." It was always shedding and always green. The children loved its many curving trunks and branches, so easy to climb up and slide down.

Joel walked on, half-dreaming, half-observing. Now he noticed that the ground was getting rougher and many trees were down, some piled on top of each other. Brush was thick and an army of briars and brambles blocked his path. To be a logger, a boy had to learn to climb steep grades, jump over logs, wade through brush and saw and chop trees. Joel wished for a chain saw like Dad's, with a sawlike blade five feet long and a small gas engine built into its handle. All he would have to do was hold it against the wood and let it buzz, as it melted its way through a tree. Some day he'd have one of his own to take with him into the woods.

Dad never went anywhere without his Homelite. If a big tree came down across the highway in a storm Dad, or the next logger coming along, would stop, buck it, and roll it over to one side. No wonder the loggers had to go to the woods armed with spiked boots, tin hat, and leather gloves. They never knew when they might meet an enemy. A fallen tree could be an enemy—a wild animal could be one, too.

There were other enemies—big rocks and boulders sliding down a steep cliff, falling snags, "widow-makers" crashing down on your head when you weren't looking, tangles of vines to trip you up, logs to stumble over. The woods was a friendly place, but it could be dangerous, too, if you weren't alert.

Suddenly the wind began to blow. It ruffled Joel's hair and blew through his cotton shirt. He felt chilly—he had been

sweating the minute before. What direction was the wind coming from? He reached for his compass, but it was not in his pocket. He tried his other pockets. The compass was gone. Oh, well, he'd get along without it. There was the sun, that was west. And the moss was always on the north side of the trees. He knew which direction he was going, all right. Down in the valley ahead somewhere was the Drum Store and his home.

He saw a tree with a nest of bees. Did it have honey in it? That old bear ought to come and find it. He walked on past—he did not want to get stung.

The wind kept on blowing.

That meant Skinner's men must stop work. All loggers had to get out of the woods when the wind blew. Too many snags to be blown down on their heads. It was impossible to fall trees in the wind. A faller could not make the tree go where he wanted it to go. Dad had said that more than once.

The loggers must be going home now. Where was the woods road? And where was Skinner's landing? Joel listened but could not hear the men or a motor—only the clicks and clacks and rattles and rustles of twigs and branches, only the whacks and bangs of broken limbs, only the rush of the wind and a sudden clap of thunder.

Was it going to rain again?

It never rained in August. August was the driest part of the year in Douglas County, the time when people had to irrigate their hayfields and their gardens, if they wanted to save their vegetables. It never rained in August. Lightning? Thunder again, would it bring lightning, to set fires in the dry-as-dust brush?

The thought of the recent fires made the boy's heart sink.

The wind blew. The sun faded, the sky turned dark. It was as if daylight had suddenly changed to night. The wind blew with stronger force.

Now the howling gale tugged at the boy's clothes, trying to tear them off. Trees fell around him. He found an open spot and crouched down by a stump. There was nothing to do but wait till the blow was over.

It grew darker. There was something moving. Was it an animal—a coyote, a cougar? Things were hiding behind trees, sometimes they peeped out. What was it? What were they? Birds, branches, animals? Oh, if he'd only brought Corky with him! That little old dog was mean, but he wasn't afraid of anything.

Joel knew he must get back to Eddie. He jumped up and started calling: *"ED—DIE! ED—DIE!"* He called over and over, but only an echo came back. If Eddie didn't hear him, surely the loggers would. No, they had stopped work when the wind began to blow. They must be halfway home by this time, maybe already there.

"ED—DIE! ED—DIE!" It was only a waste of breath.

He stood still and looked around. At the edge of the timber, he could see the sky. That was the way to go. Eddie's Fire Watch was in an open place. He took courage and ran. It was hard to run, for the vines kept tripping him and the briars kept holding him back.

What he came to was a deep ravine, one he had never seen before. The drop was so deep, he could not see the bottom. There was only a trail on the ledge, nothing to hang to above and a long way to fall below. He turned and began to run the other way, madly, anywhere to get away.

Now he had no idea where he was. Every tree, every trunk, every path looked alike. Snags and logs and rotten stumps blocked his path. Vines and thorns and briars reached out to grab him by the feet, to scratch his arms and face. Twigs and limbs and needles and leaves pelted him like stones, strange noises pounded in his ears, whistlings and sighings and grumblings and crashings and bangings and whackings . . . The woods had come alive in the terrifying gale. The boy's body became a mass of aches and pains and hurtings and fears and tears and despair.

It was nearly dark now. The night animals would soon be out, the owls with their weird screeches, the cougar with its screaming, the coyote with its long-drawn-out wail. Oh, if he could only find Eddie again . . .

Where was the Fire Watch? Had Eddie's brother come in the Model A and taken him home? Was Joel left all alone now in the forest, the forest he loved so much? Was he lost, lost for the first time in his life?

He stumbled on, not knowing or caring where he went, just to keep going. His head ached and his stomach pained with emptiness. His thoughts kept going round and round. The forest was no longer a friend, it was an enemy. It had turned on him and he hated it. How could he ever have wanted to be a logger? The forest was the logger's enemy all his life. It existed only to destroy him.

The forest was a menace, a hiding place for cruel animals, for dangerous trees that killed men or maimed them for life. How could he ever have loved it? It turned on everyone who tried to be its friend. Billy had said once of Joel's dad: "If he keeps on working in the woods, it'll get him some day. He'll get *his!*" Horrible thought—or was it a premonition?

Joel stumbled and fell full-length on the ground, sobbing. He beat the earth with his fists and cried out, "I hate you! I hate you! I hate you!" He cried until he could cry no more.

Exhausted he lay there, he never knew how long. He lay there as the gales continued to blow over him. He lay there and the woods and all else faded away as he lost consciousness. A long time afterward he stirred. Had he fallen asleep? How could he have slept when his whole world had gone mad about him? Had he slept his fears, his fatigue, his nightmares away?

He stirred and stretched. He felt strangely calm now, as if a

hard-fought battle was over at last. But still he did not open his
eyes. He did not want to come back to life, to have to face
reality.

Then he felt something, something touching his arm. It felt
like something licking him. One of the dogs, maybe. But no, he
had left Corky at home. Something *was* licking him, on the arm
below the elbow. He opened his eyes and there was a baby
fawn!

He lay still, not daring to move for fear of frightening it. Soon
it danced away and joined the mother deer. They skipped away
together.

Joel sat up and looked around.

What time was it? How long had he been lost in the woods?
The dark clouds had blown away, and the sun was shining. The
sun had not set yet. In August the twilights lasted till nine or ten
at night. How long had he been sleeping?

The blow was over. The forest was still now—peaceful and
quiet. A little red pine squirrel caught the boy's eye. Up and
down and round about it jumped, cutting down cones, scolding
and chattering. What a clown it was! Joel held out his hand and
the little fellow jumped up on it. It eyed him with its bright
little eye and began to scold. Then it jumped to a stump and
nibbled on a pine cone as big as itself.

Joel could not help laughing.

The forest was quiet again, a haven of peace and rest. He did
not want to go, but knew he must.

How? Where? Could he find the way home alone?

First he must think things out. What had Dad told him to do?
Oh, yes, how could he have forgotten? When lost in the woods,

there's just one rule to follow—*go down hill, keep going down hill. There's always a creek and a road at the bottom.*

It was a long trudge and Joel never knew how long it took him. He fell many times, but got up again and started over. Hours later he reached the valley road, and a man that he knew picked him up and drove him to the Drum Cash Store.

The store was closed for the night, but a light was on in the kitchen.

Joel hurried up the woods road to go home. He could not get there fast enough. He knew that food and bed waited for him there. He was tired as he had never been tired before, tired in every bone and muscle.

It was dark now. The long daylight had come to an end.

Funny, there were no lights on in the house. Had everybody gone to bed early?

The dogs came tearing out to meet him. All three of them jumped on him and nearly knocked him over. Joel was glad to see them, but too tired to enjoy the force of their welcome.

"Get down! Get down!" he yelled. "Let me alone, I tell you!"

Nobody came out of the house.

Why didn't somebody come? Why didn't they ask, *Where have you been? Why did you stay away so long? Don't tell me you've been lost in the woods! Don't tell me you've been lost on the mountain! Don't you know your way around better than that?*

No voices, no questions, no bawling out for getting lost.

No sisters, no Dad, no Mom.

Joel stomped into the house and switched on a light. The door

had been left wide open. No supper on the table, the table not even set. No food had been cooked on the stove.

Had Mom and the girls gone to town on a shopping spree, and forgot to come back? Had they been wrecked in the car and got killed? But Dad—where was he? He'd have come home from the woods hours ago. Where could Dad have gone?

It was too much. All this, after what he'd been through. Joel could not take any more. He'd have to find out. There was only one person who would know—Myra Ross at the store, in bed or not. She always knew everything.

Back to the highway he ran and pounded on the store door.

He waited a long time, then pounded again. "Let me in!" he shouted.

At last, Myra called out, "Who's there?"

"Me, Joel Bartlett!" he answered. "Let me in, I say!"

Myra opened the door and said, "So it's you. Fine time o' night for a kid like you to be comin' home."

"Where's my folks?" demanded Joel. "I come home and there's nobody there. No supper and the door wide open."

"Worse things than that can happen," said Myra, grimly. "Come in and sit down."

"Where's my folks?" demanded Joel, his voice still louder.

"Don't wake up the whole neighborhood," said Myra.

She had a bright red dressing gown on, and a frilly cap over her curly hair. She looked as if she had been sleeping and was still only half-awake.

She took Joel by the hand and pulled him in. She pulled him into the kitchen and told him to sit down.

"Where's my folks . . ."

"You had anything to eat?" she asked.

The boy shook his head. "What I want to know is . . ."

Myra went slowly to the icebox, fixed a plate of cold meat and cheese and put it in front of him. She laid out some slices of bread and poured a big glass of milk.

"Now, eat!" she said. "When that's all gone, I'll talk to you."

Joel was hungry all right, so it did not take him long to gobble the food.

Myra sat by, half-asleep, and watched him.

"You sure were hungry," she said.

"You'd be hungry, too," began Joel, "if you . . ." Then he stopped. He'd never tell *her* what had happened to him.

"You look kinda ragged and beat up," said Myra.

Joel shut his mouth tight. He'd never tell *her,* no matter how much she hinted. He'd never hear the end of it if *she* knew.

"I asked you . . ." he began.

"Yes, yes," said Myra, "and I guess I might as well tell you. You got to know sooner or later. Your dad got hurt in the woods today."

She said it in a quiet voice as if it was nothing at all.

Joel's face went white and he began to shake all over.

Dad got hurt . . . it couldn't be true. *Not Dad. Not Dad. Nothing ever happened to Dad.* Joel's world went topsy-turvy again.

"What'd you say?" asked Joel, when he could speak.

"Your dad got hurt," said Myra calmly. "They took him to Medford Hospital in the ambulance. Your mom and the girls drove down to be with him. They'll stay there till they find out how he's gettin' along—a few days, maybe longer."

Joel gasped. He could not believe it.

"He hurt bad?" He managed to get the words out.

"How should I know?" said Myra.

"Didn't they . . ." Then he stopped.

"You're to stay here, your mom said," Myra went on.

"Here?" asked Joel. "Me sleep here?"

"Yes," said Myra.

Chapter Ten

THE TREASURE

IT was hard getting used to the fact that Dad was in the hospital. Mom went several times a week to visit him and often Jinx and Sandy went along. But Joel refused to go.

"Got things to do at home," he growled.

The hard part was hearing everybody ask about Dad, and listening to their comments.

They said: "Every logger gets it. He had it coming. He went scot-free too long."

"We all have to go some time. If we're careless, we may go sooner."

"No logger goes till his time comes!"

"Big Joe's been mighty lucky! His luck couldn't hold."

"Accidents don't just *happen*. There's always a cause, you know."

It hurt Joel's pride that Dad was helpless in the hospital, and not out in the woods doing a strong man's work.

And of course, Billy Weber, even Billy, Joel's best friend, had to rub it in.

"I told you he'd get *his* one of these days," said Billy darkly. "I told you every logger's got all his bones broke."

"Shut up!" shouted Joel.

Dad's previous accidents, his concussions and his broken ribs and noses—all these were nothing. It was the real thing this time, so bad Joel could not talk about it. Dad was on the critical list at the hospital.

He could not admit it to Billy, but maybe Billy was right and Dad had really got *his*.

No! Joel would not even think about it. He remembered what a strong man Dad was. He'd pull through, sure, just as he had so many times before. Joel just *had* to believe that.

Joel wished Mom would stop talking about the accident. But she had to tell her story over and over. Joel heard it so often he felt as if he had been there himself.

The humidity was so low that Monday, Mom had expected Dad home early. He ought to appear any time, but he didn't. It got later and later. Still he did not come. Where was he? Why didn't he come? She drove the old Ford down to the store to find out.

Then the crummy pulled up without him.

"What's happened?" Mom asked. "Where's Big Joe?"

"He stayed to work on the shovel," Al Duncan told her. "He'll be back later."

So Mom started for home. Just as she turned in at the woods

road, an ambulance whizzed by, the siren screaming. Mom went right back to the store. Everybody was buzzing around to find out who had been hurt. But nobody told her anything. They knew it all the time, but were too cowardly to tell her.

So she went home. Dad wasn't there. It was way past time for him to come home. He never stopped at the tavern the way a lot of loggers did. He always came straight home. But where was he? He didn't come.

Even when you know it's going to come, you are never prepared, she told herself. Why be afraid? Big Joe is a logger. I knew it when I married him. I've got to live with it. The loggers' wives were all alike. They hated logging, but the men were stubborn and kept on loving it. The loggers' wives, Mom told herself, and even their children lived *under the shadow of fear*. It was no way to live, she'd get Big Joe out of the woods, take him away to the city . . . but she knew he'd never go. Even the children—there was Jinx crying her eyes out because Dad had not come home . . .

Somebody was at the door. It was Uncle Irv, Mom's brother. His face was white, so she knew before he spoke.

"That was HIM in the ambulance!" she managed to say.

Irv nodded and put his arms around her. Jinx and Sandy came and they all cried and sobbed together.

Irv told them what he knew, but it wasn't much.

"A widow-maker came down, hit him on the head and tore the muscles of his shoulder," said Irv. "He saw it coming and stepped back, but the wind started blowing right then and it swerved over and got him."

So Dad was on the critical list. There was nerve injury, the doctor said and other effects. It was terrible to listen to all the details. Dad, the fearless high climber, not afraid of any- thing, was down in bed and nobody knew when he'd get up again.

Life at home was not the same without Dad. Days and weeks passed by somehow, one just like the other. All the spice had gone out of daily living. A heavy cloud hung over the home, the cloud of fear and anxiety.

Uncle Irv and Uncle Curt brought their families to visit, but even Mom wished they would go away. She did not want sym- pathy. It was bad enough not knowing if Dad would ever get well again, without listening to the doubtful words of sympathy that even her kinfolk tried to give. Everybody said it was a blessing he did not get hit on the spine. That was the worst of all, it meant paralysis.

Mom complained about the trips to the hospital.

"I'm wearing my tires out, putting on so much mileage," she said. "Fifty miles each way and all those pesky curves on that mountain. I wish I never had to drive it again."

One day when she came back, she sounded more cheerful. Uncle Irv had stopped in, and Joel came up to hear her report.

"I found out what's botherin' Joe," she told Uncle Irv. "He's worried about money."

Uncle Irv smiled. "Him with the highest-paid job in the woods! That makes me laugh!"

Joel knew that all loggers were heavily insured, and that the insurance covered accidents on the job. It paid hospital and doctor bills and 25 per cent of a man's wages.

"Well," said Mom, "there's payments due on a number of

things, this living room set and . . ."

Irv interrupted. He looked at the chairs and davenport. "They're not paid for yet?" he asked. "Why, they're wore out already."

The two big dogs jumped off the davenport and part of the stuffing fell on the floor. Joel picked it up and tried to push it back in.

"What Joe gets from the insurance will just about pay for the groceries," said Mom. "School's opening soon and the kids all need new school clothes."

"Nellie, you always were a spendthrift," said Irv. "Don't you ever save anything when going's good? When you gonna learn to save a few pennies?"

Mom went on. "But what's on Joe's mind is the timber. If the taxes are not paid, he'll lose the timber."

Irv frowned. "That's a horse of a different color. The kids can go to school in rags . . ."

"Not me!" broke in Sandy. "I'll be in first year High. I got to look decent. I need a new skirt and a coat and . . ."

Uncle Irv turned on the girl in anger.

"Well, you're not going to get them!" he said. "If your Mom's too soft to bawl you out, your Uncle Irv will have to do it. You can stop being selfish and think of someone else for a while."

Sandy subsided in teen-age tears.

Jinx came up and sat on Uncle Irv's lap.

"Could I get a job, Uncle Irv?" she asked. "I'd help pay for the davenport. I've got five dollars from peeling poles and twenty dollars of my prize money."

Joel reached out and kicked her on the shin.

"Stop showin' off!" he growled. "Nobody'd hire a silly galoot like you! Besides, what could you *do*?"

Jinx turned on Joel and pounded him with her fists. Mom shooed them both out into the yard. The dogs leaped on them and began a frantic barking.

It was after a visit from Dot Kramer that Mom got her big idea.

"We'll go cone picking," she said firmly. "We can pick and sell enough cones to pay the taxes, pay up on the living-room set, and meet those bills at Penney's and Ward's."

"You mean go up in the deep woods and pick cones and drag 'em down?" asked Sandy. "You won't catch me helping. Donna and Sherry Kramer told me what nasty work it is. You get covered with pitch from head to foot."

Nobody listened to Sandy.

Jinx was eager to go, always ready for new adventure. Girls of her age did not get to the woods as often as boys, or as often as they wanted to go.

But it was hard for Joel. He had a difficult decision to make. After his experience in the big blow, he never wanted to go to the woods again. Getting lost was no joke. He had never told anyone what happened. No one had noticed that anything was wrong except Myra Ross, and he had never told her a word. She had not asked questions, either, thank goodness. Nobody knew a thing about it. They had all been concerned over Dad's accident.

Joel did not want to go back to the woods. It was a terrible place, the forest was an enemy. It destroyed everybody who loved it. Look what a beating it gave him when he got lost, look what it did to all the loggers, breaking their bones, look what it did to Dad, half-killing him. Joel was through with the woods, his mind was made up. He would never be a logger and spend his life in the woods.

Then, too, this was funny business, Mom going to the woods, Mom who had never even seen Dad fall a tree, let alone top one, who didn't know a donkey from a shovel and who hated everything about logging. Nobody could even *drag* her to the woods up to now. Was all this just talk? Or did she mean what she said? It sounded phony—Mom who never saved a penny in her life was now going to pay off all the debts and taxes!

"I won't go!" said Joel firmly.

"But, Joel, you love the woods . . ." Mom began.

"I'm not going!" shouted Joel, angrily. *"Nobody can make me!"*

"Oh, if only Dad were here," said Mom, half crying.

But she went ahead anyhow. She went to the Forest Service and got her cone-picking permit. The Forest Service would buy the cones for the seeds in them. The cones had to be closed, with seeds still inside. When the cones opened up, they shed the seeds and were no good. The Forest Service used the seeds for replanting. They paid four dollars a bushel for Douglas fir cones, and more for smaller ones. The best cones were to be found at high elevations, above thirty-five hundred feet. The fall was the season for cone picking, late September, October, and November, up to Thanksgiving. They had to be picked before frost.

Mom went ahead with her plans. Uncle Irv said she could use his pick-up and Dot Kramer was to go along the first time to show her where to go.

Next morning, Mom and the girls dressed in their oldest shirts and jeans. They tied scarves around their heads. They hunted up heavy gloves to wear and put buckets and gunnysacks in the truck. Mom packed a basket of lunch.

They all piled in the truck and Joel watched them drive off.

Were they really going? Joel could not believe it. Mom was a greenhorn in the woods. So were Jinx and Sandy. Mom did not know a bobcat from a cougar, a sugar pine from an oak, a bat from an owl, a snag from a living tree, a chipmunk from a flying squirrel. How could a woman like that make out in the woods? The girls were soft, too. Picking cones was hard work, not just play like picking wild flowers for a bouquet. Sacks of cones were heavy—who was going to lift them?

They needed a man with them—or at least a boy.

Suddenly Joel could not bear to be left behind. He tore down the woods road as fast as he could go.

They had stopped at the store to meet Dot Kramer. She started ahead in her own car, and Mom stepped on the gas to follow. Joel was just in time. He jumped in the cab beside Mom. The girls were in the back. Soon they left the highway and went rocking and bumping along a side road into the woods.

Mom looked at Joel, but said nothing.

Sandy sulked in a corner, because she didn't want to go. Jinx teased her and that made her crosser than ever. Dot Kramer took them on a devious route, around many curves and corners and up and down over hills and valleys. Joel had no idea where they were, when at last they came to a stop. It was impossible to drive any farther. The so-called road just disappeared. They all climbed out.

Dot looked up at the steep hill in front of them.

"Here we are!" she cried. "Now let's see who can be the first one to get to the top. The higher you go, the better the cones!"

Sandy looked up aghast.

"You mean we're going to climb this *mountain?*" she asked.

"It's only a hill, Sandy," said Mom.

"Sandy, you sound just like my girls," said Dot Kramer. "Donna and Sherry are getting so fat and lazy, they can't even . . ."

"I'm not fat and I'm not lazy!" said Sandy.

She started up the incline. Tennis shoes with rubber soles made climbing easy. Jinx and Joel followed.

"Hey, come back!" called Mom. "Take these buckets and gunnysacks with you."

Jinx and Joel came back, but Sandy didn't.

She was already at the top when the others got there, huffing and puffing. They dropped their load and waited for Dot and Mom with the lunch basket. The minute it appeared, Sandy reached for a sandwich.

"Not yet!" scolded Dot. "We'll pick cones for three hours, then you can eat. You'll be *hungry* then!"

"I'm gonna pick sugar-pine cones," said Sandy. "They're nice and big. I'll get a bushel quick."

The cones from the sugar pines were the largest, over a foot in length, and the most beautiful. It would not take many to make a bushel.

"The best ones are those from the Douglas fir," said Dot, "about four inches long. They're worth four dollars a bushel. If you really want to make money, find a hemlock tree. Their cones are only an inch long, but they're worth seven dollars a bushel. It takes a long time to get a bushel."

"We'll raid the squirrels," Dot went on. "They like to hide the cones in damp places, where a small trickle of water comes down, all soft and mossy. Not fast running water. Look under old rotten logs and in stumps, too. Some are even buried underground."

They all scattered out to look.

It was Mom who found the first big cache. On a damp mossy bank, at the base of an incline, she found piles of cones under some rotten logs. Dot pulled a few out and tested them by cutting them down through the center. They were full of seeds.

"Good going!" she said. "Get 'em all! Clean 'em out!"

Jinx and Joel came and helped Mom scoop them up in buck-

ets. The bank was packed solid for a long distance. They emptied the buckets into the gunnysacks and went back for more. At
last they had them all. Their gloves and arms and clothes were
sticky with pitch.

"Poor little old squirrels," said Jinx. "Will they starve if we
take all their seeds away?"

"There's plenty more on the trees," said Mom. "They'll just
have to work a little harder and get in a new supply."

"Keep going higher!" advised Dot. "The higher you go, the
better the cones."

They kept on climbing up and up. Actually, the work was fun.
The day was perfect, cool and pleasant, the sun not too hot. Joel
tried to figure out where a squirrel would hide cones. It was like
trying to enter a squirrel's mind and think as he thought. This

helped him to find cones in unexpected places.

Dot said, "Joel, you're a regular squirrel yourself, you're bringing so many cones in."

I'm robbing the squirrels, thought Joel. He looked overhead, where they were jumping and scolding in the branches. *We won't take them all, we'll leave plenty for you, you won't starve, don't worry!*

His biggest haul was inside an old rotten log. It had been a mighty tree once. Now its full length, seventy feet or more, lay on the ground rotting, going back to Mother Earth. The entire heart was hollow—and packed solid with cones.

Joel stared at the beautiful cache—treasure for the taking. After all her rebuffs, after all her cruelty, was the forest giving back of her bounty, to heal the boy's wounds?

A little red pine squirrel chattered on a branch overhead. He began cutting off cones and dropping them into the hollow log. Joel grinned. Why, the squirrels weren't scolding. They were *helping* him! They were his *friends!* He laughed as a shower of cones came down into his bucket.

Sandy, who could not locate any caches at all, came and helped scoop the cones out of the big log and fill the sacks. There was no end to the supply. After the sacks were full, Joel found some sugar-pine cones. He shook the seeds out, cracked and ate them. He gave some to Sandy. They were delicious, with a woodsy taste. He liked them as much as the squirrels did.

Soon Dot Kramer left them to go home, after giving directions for their return to the highway. After Dot left, Mom said they could stop, rest a while, and eat lunch. Where was Jinx?

"Jinx! Jinx Bartlett!" Mom called and called.

But the girl did not come.

"I hope she did not go and get lost," said Joel. The word meant more to him now than it ever had before.

"Joel, go find her," said Mom, as she spread the picnic lunch on a cloth on the ground.

"Gosh!" cried Joel. "What if she's LOST?"

"I told you, go find her," said Mom.

Joel hesitated, then started off. He began to call, *"Yoo-hoo! Yoo-hoo!"* when he heard a faint answer. Or, was it just an echo?

"Yoo-hoo! Jin - n - n - x!" he called again.

"Here I am!" came the answer.

He ran over and found her, sitting on a stump, crying.

"I didn't know which way to go," she said. "I heard something, it growled, I think it was a bear . . . I got SPOOKED!"

"Aw, come on," said Joel. "Mom and Sandy are eating lunch. It'll all be gone if you don't hurry."

In the afternoon they moved up higher, following Dot's advice. Going was rough, but the caches were smaller and it took longer to fill the sacks. Handling the cones was a messy job, as they dripped sticky pitch over hands and clothing. There were no encounters with wild animals. Joel was disappointed. He had no chance to be a hero.

Then came the task of closing and tying the sacks and filling out the Forest Service labels. Dot had shown Mom just how to do it. Each sack had to be labeled with the elevation, the location, and the type of tree. Mom left two ears at the top sack corners for handholds. The hardest part of all was getting the sacks down the mountainside to the truck. They were heavy. The sacks of dry cones weighed at least forty pounds. If the cones were wet, they weighed as much as sixty or seventy.

Mom tried to do it the way Dot showed her. She lifted a sack onto her back, holding onto the ears over each shoulder. Joel did the same. Jinx and Sandy could not even lift the lightest sack, so they pulled them. They started down the steep incline.

"If I stumble," said Mom, gaily, "the sack will turn a somersault and land at the bottom of the canyon!"

"So will you!" added Joel. "So watch out."

Mom was trying to be cheerful, but it was hard work for her and Joel knew it. How determined she was, even when the work was so difficult. Joel admired her spunk. Of course, she was

doing it for Dad! That made all the difference. Joel would never have come to the woods himself today if it had not been for Dad. It was a way to help Dad.

They took the bags down part way, then came back for more. The girls helped all they could, and finally, by lifting and pulling and tugging, they got them down to the place where the pick-up stood. After a rest, they hoisted them up.

It was a good haul for their first attempt. Mom was pleased, but she was too tired to cook supper when they got home. The girls had to put cold food on the table.

"We'll go every day now," Mom said, "and after school starts, we can keep on going on Saturdays."

Sandy groaned, but Jinx clapped her hands.

It made Joel happy inside.

It was something they could all do for Dad, instead of sitting around feeling sorry for themselves.

Chapter Eleven

THE CHOICE

"OH, it's raining! It's pouring!" cried Jinx, going out on the porch.

"We can't go to town today," said Sandy.

But Mom said, "We're going anyhow."

The rains came and stopped everything.

It was early November and the rains would go on for six months, the same wet soaking rains that had fed the roots of the giant trees for centuries, the rains that had watered the forests since the beginning of time.

The rains came and washed everything away.

After the long dry spell, the rains did not soak into the bone-dry ground. They just washed off. They washed out the roots of trees, making them fall over in the slightest wind. When gusts came, snags went toppling, sliding over the steep slopes and crisscrossing the highways. The rains loosened rocks on cliffsides and washed out gravel and boulders.

The rains came and stopped everything.

Logging stopped. The men went home disgusted. They holed up for the winter, drawing unemployment compensation checks. Lowboy trailers hauled the equipment off locations, all the donkeys and shovels and rigging, all the cats and cables and chokers and everything else. Logging came to an abrupt halt for another year.

No more working in the woods, no more logs on the landings. No more logs in huge logging trucks to be crowding the highways and dumped off at the millponds at the mills in town. The highways were quiet and deserted now, with only a few straggling cars.

The whole world seemed to have come to an end.

At the Bartlett house, the rains washed down the hill where Dad had logged off the trees and the road he had bladed out with his bulldozer. The rains turned the slope into a sea of mud. The dooryard became a pigpen. Mud stuck to everybody's shoes and was carried into the house.

But nobody cared. Nobody even noticed it. It was not a dreary day, but a happy one, because Mom went to town and brought Dad home.

Yes, Dad was home at last. After all the long weary weeks of lying in bed at the hospital, after all the doctors and surgery and medicines and therapies, after all the worry and anxiety and tedious waiting, Dad was home again.

Even the dogs were glad! When Dad first stepped out of the

car, the dogs leaped upon him to show their welcome.

"Down Ringo! Down, Corky! Down, Rex!" shouted Dad. "I know you're all glad to see me, but . . . don't knock me over!"

After he went inside, the dogs followed him, barking and yowling and whining.

Inside, Jinx and Sandy fell on their dad and smothered him with hugs and kisses. Joel just stood and smiled.

"Down, girls, down!" shouted Dad. "You're as bad as the dogs. Don't knock me over."

There were mud tracks all over the floor, but Mom didn't scold. Dad went to the davenport and sat down. He wasn't strong and husky now. He was thin and white and weak. Though greatly changed, he was still the same old dad. The children crowded round. There was only one thing that mat-

tered now—Dad was well and home again.

"Where's my cork shoes?" he asked the first thing. He grinned at Mom. "You didn't throw them out, Nellie, did you?"

"No," said Mom. "Joel wouldn't let me. He kept them safe for you in his own room. He wouldn't even let me touch them."

Joel brought them out, all shiny and well-greased. Dad put them on again.

"Just to see how they feel!" he said, with a laugh. "I've almost forgotten."

He got up and strode across the floor. The calks made holes in the linoleum.

Mom cried out, "Look, Joe! See what you're doing!"

"Don't gripe, Nellie," said Dad softly. "These little old cork boots will be buyin' you a new carpet one o' these days."

Mom smiled. It hurt her to know that Dad was going back to logging again, but she knew it was bound to come. Even getting half-killed was not going to stop him. Logging was the very breath of his life.

"No more logging!" cried Sandy. "Now we can move to town and stay there."

"Who told you that?" asked Jinx.

"Nobody," said Sandy. "But with Dad nearly killed, he sure can't go on logging!"

"Can't I?" Dad laughed.

"You are going back to logging again, aren't you, Dad?" asked Joel.

"Sure thing," said Dad. "Not right now. I got all winter to get my strength back. Doc says I'll be as good as new, time spring comes and logging starts again. That day can't come too soon."

"Oh, Daddy, you're not SPOOKED?" cried Jinx, eyes open wide.

"SPOOKED?" Dad roared with laughter. "Of course not."

Joel said slowly, "There's always *danger*, Dad."

Dad looked at the boy as if he knew what was in his mind.

"Men don't think of it as danger, son," he said, in a kindly voice. "They know what they are doing. They follow one rule: *Just make sure you are in the clear.*"

Joel did not answer.

"That's about right, ain't it, son?"

Joel nodded.

"It's *work!*" Dad went on. "You can't be afraid of work or you'd better stay out of the woods. It takes a man's strength, all his soul and body . . . He works like the devil . . . he gives all he's got to give, and even sometimes that don't seem to be enough . . . Sometimes he has to pay the price . . ."

Suddenly the house shook and gave a lurch. Then it began to slide. Dishes fell off the table, chairs slid, and Jinx tumbled over on the floor.

"The house! It's sliding!" cried Mom, holding onto the door-frame. Then she added, trying to smile, "I know it's not an earthquake this time!"

The house had stood still all through the dry summer. They had almost forgotten it could slide. Now the heavy rains had undermined the foundations and dislodged the posts Dad had put in last spring. It slid a foot or two, then stopped.

"Good!" cried Joel, relieved. "I thought we were going to land in the creek, but we didn't." Everybody laughed.

"Glory!" cried Jinx. "I'm gettin' outa here!"

She ran for the door. But Dad pulled her back.

"It's rainin' cats and dogs outside," he said. "Stay in here and keep dry."

The house lurched again and everybody laughed.

"But I tell you," said Mom, half crying, "it's no laughing matter . . ."

The next minute Dad had his arms around her.

"As soon as the rain stops, Nellie, I'll fix it," he said. "In fact, I'm plannin' to . . ." but he did not tell all his dreams.

They sat down again. Mom put the coffee pot on the stove and got out some cookies. It was like Christmas and birthdays and picnics and Fourth of July all put together—just having Dad at home again.

Mom poured a big cup of coffee for Dad, then told him the news—that the bills were all paid up, even the living-room set was paid for. It surprised Dad so, he spilled half his coffee and it splashed all over the davenport.

Jinx ran to get a cloth to wipe it up.

"You mean it's OURS now?" cried Dad, patting the cushions. "Really OURS?"

"Yes," said Mom. "All paid for."

"Then it don't matter if we spill coffee on it!" Dad roared with laughter.

But he did not want to listen when Mom started talking about the taxes.

"Don't rub it in," he said, getting angry. "I'll do what I can, as soon as I can. No man can do more."

"Oh, but Dad!" cried Sandy. "We all helped. We gave Mom all our savings, what we made from peeling poles and . . ."

"And my Rooster Crow prize money," said Jinx. "I decided I didn't want a mustang from Wyoming, after all. I couldn't figure out how to get it here all the way from Wyoming and besides, I could never break a wild horse, so . . . I'll just keep on ridin' old Star up to the range, even if I do get saddle sore."

Dad put his arm around her. "You gave up your prize money?"

"We didn't want you to lose Granddad's timber," said Joel.

Not till Mom showed Dad the tax receipt would he believe her. Then he could not understand it. How could a woman and three kids have done such a thing? Impossible!

"There's something phony about this," he said.

Joel was tickled to see how puzzled Dad was.

"It was not a miracle, Dad," Joel said. "We just worked hard."

Then the whole story of the cone picking came out and of the bushels and bushels of cones picked and sacked and labeled and loaded and hauled to the Forest Service. The whole story of the hard climbs to the high elevations and all the bruises and bumps and bee-stings and dirt and pitch and ruined jeans and hard, hard work; and how when they tried to outwit the squirrels, the little old buggers set to and *helped* them!

Dad laughed to hear it all. He said it was "good medicine for a sick man" but he wasn't sick anymore. The timber, Granddad's beautiful timber, was saved and Dad had a big winter ahead, with all the things he planned to do.

"But you have to rest for six months, the doctor said," Mom reminded him.

"Rest?" cried Dad. "My eye! That doctor never met a logger before. That's all that's the matter with *him.*"

There was no holding Dad back.

As soon as the rains slowed up, as if they might quit, Dad got Curt and Irv over to help him. He did the directing and they did the work. They jacked the old log house up and moved it back to its original foundations. They did a better job this time, guaranteed to keep the building where it belonged.

Then they started the new job that Dad had not talked about. They poured cement for foundations for a *new* house, back farther up the hill on a level spot where nothing could be washed off. Mom was to have her new house at last.

For the first few weeks after Dad's return, neighbors and friends and relatives kept coming in to see Dad, to talk and visit. The men were idle now and so it was a great time for visiting.

Uncle Curt and Uncle Irv and their families came often, and Aunt Alice and Uncle Bob came over from Rogue River with their children. The Kramers and the Duncans and the Watsons and the Carters dropped in, as well as others. Everybody wanted to be reassured that Big Joe Bartlett was a good as new again. They left, after each visit, without any doubts.

But it was Eddie Wykoff's visit that cheered Joel the most. It was Eddie who helped him to think things through and come to some important conclusions.

Eddie talked to Dad for a while, and then he and Joel went back off up the hill into the woods. They walked, and talked as they went along. The forest was quieter now, with the approach of winter, as if it were getting ready for a long rest. Only a few squirrels and chipmunks were out. Because it was the hunting season, even the deer had made themselves scarce. Neither Eddie nor Joel carried guns.

Joel did most of the talking and Eddie listened. Joel found it easy to talk to Eddie. Eddie looked upon Joel, not as a little kid, but as a boy of his own age. He made him feel like an equal.

Logging and cutting down trees had been a part of Joel's life for as long as he could remember. He had never questioned. He loved the woods and its plants and wildlife. He loved all the animals that made their homes there and were happy and contented there.

At the same time, he loved man's machines. As a little boy, he liked all the machines that ran by themselves, the beat-up old car that Dad drove to town, the tractor that plowed people's fields, the truck that hauled things, especially the big logging truck that hauled the giant logs. It was Joel who wanted to drive a logging truck and Billy Weber who wanted to drive a cat. For the logging machines—the donkey, the shovel, and the beloved cat were the best of all.

Now for the first time Joel began to realize things. He had never thought of it before, but now he could see it plainly. He realized that these two opposing forces could never meet, that Mother Nature was pulling in one way and man and his machines in another. Man and his machines were out to destroy nature.

"Oh, I wouldn't say that . . ." began Eddie.

"Wait," said Joel. "That's not all."

He told how he had loved to watch a big tree fall, but now he knew that every tree that fell left an empty place behind it; that the place where it had once stood and lifted its branches and leaves to the rain and the sun was now just bleak emptiness. Now he could see that the thin soil in the cracks on the steep mountainsides, where the tree's roots had clung to hidden rocks and deep moisture so tenaciously, was being washed off down into the canyon, and that the little seedling trees would never have anything there to take hold of. Now he could see the stripped mountainside as a scene of desolation. In the place where the great proud trees had once stood in their green and growing grandeur, all that was left was a desert of ugliness.

"I hate the Forest Service!" cried Joel. "Every time I see a

clear-cut, I wonder if they've gone crazy."

"No," said Eddie. "They know what they are doing."

"Oh, yeah?" said Joel, remembering Dad's angry words that day in the woods. "They read it out of a book?"

"Their methods are scientific," Eddie explained. "Tree farming is a science."

"Why can't they do more salvage logging and do it without wrecking all the little trees?" asked Joel. "Why can't they leave the best trees to reseed themselves? The loggers say that seeds planted by nature grow better and faster than those dropped by a man from a helicopter—those that fall on 'dry ground and never sprout for lack of moisture, or in tangles of thorns and briars where they get choked out.' "

"But remember," Eddie said, " 'some fall on good ground, too, and bring forth good fruit.' " Then he added, "Many Forest sales specify salvage logging. Some salvage units are being logged for the third time—to keep all dead wood and snags out, and this keeps insects out, too."

"I hate them for all their spraying," said Joel. "They're killing off the wildlife . . . Anything that eats a tree seed they call an enemy of the forest. They're disturbing the balance of nature."

Eddie told him all he knew about the Forest Service practices.

Then Joel said solemnly: "I've wanted to be a logger all my life, Eddie, but now I know I can't ever be one. For a while I hated the woods, but now I can see it was only because I love it so much. I feel disloyal to my dad—it all means so much to him. But I know now I cannot spend my life sawing down big trees, destroying Mother Nature. I just can't."

"Why not plant them then?" asked Eddie quietly.

Joel stared at him.

"What do you mean?"

"You can spend your life planting trees instead of sawing them down," said Eddie.

"Aw, be a little Johnny Appleseed, eh?" scoffed Joel, with a grin. "Is that what you mean?"

"How old are you now, Joel?"

"Twelve," said Joel. "Thirteen come spring."

"You got to keep on at school and get a good education," said Eddie. "That's important if you join the Forest Service."

"Join the Forest Service?" shouted Joel. "Who's gonna join that bunch of idiots? I told you I hate them. I hate their clear-cuts, their spraying, their crazy helicopter seeding and every other darn thing they do. Dad says they're just a bunch of crazy college guys . . ."

"That's right," said Eddie. "You'll have to save up and go to college, same as I'm doin'. There's lots of summer jobs you can get, peeling poles, picking cones and oh, yes, when you're fifteen, you can be Fire Watch."

Joel did not speak.

"You'll make a good one," said Eddie. "You know the woods so well, a hundred times better than I did when I started."

"I could be Fire Watch?" asked Joel, listening carefully.

Good thing Eddie didn't know about him getting lost that day in the big blow and how he got home that night.

"Sure," said Eddie. "I'll tell the Forest Service. They'll be glad to hear about you. You can learn a lot from them."

Eddie paused. "I'm not gonna be a logger, either," he said slowly. "One log rollin' over my foot is enough. I'm lucky I ain't got a wooden leg. That one log made me change my mind quick. Have you heard the old saying: 'Better a live coward than a dead hero?' Well, I'm yellow and not ashamed of it. I'm plumb scared of logging and I'll have no part in it."

Deserting Dad's job was not quite so awful for Joel if Eddie was doing it, too.

"What are you gonna do then, if you're not gonna be a logger?" asked Joel.

"Why, I'm joinin' the Forest Service, of course!" said Eddie, with a laugh. "Gonna git me a purty green uniform and stroll around in the woods all day and tell them loggers what they can and can't do. Or maybe I'll ride in one of them helicopters all summer, sprinklin' Douglas fir seeds over the countryside. Of course I got to study up some and go to college for a while. How about it, Joel? Ain't that better than losin' a leg or gettin' bopped on my tin hat?"

Joel agreed. He had to laugh.

"Heck, Eddie, you got me turned clear upside down with your crazy ideas. I start out hatin' the Forest Service and you get me wantin' to join 'em. Maybe you're right. If I'm not gonna be a logger, I got to do something—go to college first, I suppose." He thought for a minute. "But how'll I ever tell Dad? He wants me to be a logger so bad, it'll kill him for sure."

"I doubt it," said Eddie. "Your dad's weathered worse storms than this in his life. I think he can take it."

Eddie had to go.

After he left, Joel called the dogs and went for a walk in the woods. He walked and walked and ran with the dogs until he was tired. How wonderful it was, all the trees and animals and growing things. He would not have to leave it, after all. The forest was in his blood. He felt at home in the woods again.

As Eddie predicted, talking to Dad wasn't so hard, after all.

"Well, Dad," said Joel, "I've made my choice. I guess I don't want any cork boots, after all."

Dad looked up suspiciously.

"You been wantin' 'em for a long time, son," said Dad, "ever since you was knee-high to a grasshopper."

Dad and Joel had a good talk and came to the same conclusion. Dad swore at the Forest Service and called their men idiots and nitwits and college boys and other things.

"It's time they got a good sensible kid like you in there, to help run things," said Dad. "You know more about the woods and trees and wildlife than all the rest of them put together. If they'd get loggers' sons in there, maybe they could bring back the beautiful forests to the state of Oregon. Maybe they could replant all those trees that Granddad and his generation cut down!"

Joel told Dad about his talk with Eddie, and how Eddie had helped him to decide not to be a logger, after all.

"I expect you're right, son," said Dad. "Ever since you were born, I've wanted you to be a logger, and you seemed to take to it like a duck to water. A father wants his son to be like him, only better. Then somehow, down there in the hospital, things began to look different to me. All I could see ahead was the end of logging as it's been done in the past. There won't be much in it for you, time you're grown."

"That's what I'm afraid of, Dad," said Joel.

"The logging of the past is on its way out," Dad went on. "Good timber's getting harder and harder to find. Even in the National Forests, there's not much left they want cut out. There won't be many trees left to cut, time you're a man. If you're lookin' ahead for your whole lifetime, loggin's not a livelihood to choose."

"I hate to disappoint you, Dad," said Joel.

"That's O.K.," said Dad. "It's been a good life and I've loved it. I've never wanted to do anything else and I still don't. When I was young, all the forest was there, an inexhaustible supply, waiting to be cut down. That's not true anymore. Guess the lumber companies were too greedy. Now the supply's nearly gone and we need young fellers like you to replant and bring the forests back to Oregon."

"I'll do what I can, Dad," said Joel.

"Your mom will be pleased," said Dad. "She never liked logging."

"Yes, she'll be happy now," said Joel.

"But me, I'm still a logger," said Dad. "I can't wait to get back to the woods. That timber of Granddad's is still waiting for me. I like to think about it—*the trees are still there!* We've saved 'em. Granddad's trees! Maybe I won't cut 'em after all!"

"The trees are still there!" said Joel.